FALLEN
THE ADVENTURES
OF A DEEP WATER LEAF

Written and Illustrated By
Claire M. Perkins

Dear Kathi,
Dive deep, dream true,
awaken and remember YOU
:)

Clair

Intuitive Journey Press

ISBN: 978-0-9821056-2-7 (Hardcover)
ISBN: 978-1-62747-410-8
ISBN: 978-1-62747-562-4 (eBook)

DEDICATION

This book is for those who dreamed the first dream
and we who dream it forward;
for those who are stuck
and those who've learned to harness the wind;
for the deep-divers and shapeshifters
who light our way home;
and for all who chose to fall
and to forget.
It is time to awaken.
It is time to remember.

ACKNOWLEDGMENTS

This book has been a slow-growing tree. The seed was planted in a long-ago dream when the phrase "deep water leaf" was given to me as the key to healing and awakening. Years later, that seed germinated in the dark, loamy soil of deep grief, sending down roots, seeking deeper understanding. So my acknowledgments must begin with deep gratitude to my dreams (which connect me to my own higher self who lives in the Dreaming Tree) and to my son, Cameron (whose life and death pushed me to face my deepest fears and take my own deep dive to remember who I really am).

Several more years passed before the first tentative shoots and leaves emerged shyly into the sun during a "Writing as a State of Active Dreaming" workshop with Robert Moss. It was there that my main character began to speak to me. During the course of the five-day retreat, a short, poetic, three-act drama emerged. On the last day of the workshop, the group enacted a wild and rowdy rendition of it as dream theater. The opening chapters of the story came alive for me that day.

It is with great gratitude that I acknowledge Robert Moss and my fellow "Mosswood Creatives" who participated in the writing workshop with me. Thank you so much for providing the welcome sunlight that was needed to coax the seedling story into life.

Still more years passed. The seedling's tiny leaves continued to whisper in the breeze of my subconscious, sometimes quietly and sometimes with great bluster. At last it found the deep watering it thirsted for in Tom Bird's weekend writing retreat and publishing program. Tom's method for writing from the divine author within finally broke down whatever barriers there had been and the little seedling burst into abundant life, growing strong and tall and full.

I am extremely grateful to Tom Bird and his staff, who helped to bring the book to life and give it form. And I thank all of my fellow "Wave" writers, some of whom I got to know better than others, but all of whom created a wave of writing energy and passion that kept us all moving forward and provided the water and food my seedling story needed to grow into full life.

Many of the lessons my protagonist, Alora, learns on her journey reflect the lessons that have most profoundly impacted my own life journey. Lucia Capacchione, KC Miller, Robert Moss, Barbara Marx Hubbard—thank you all for the light you bring into the world through your teachings.

Each of you, in your own way, has helped me and countless others to find our way back to who we truly are.

I want to thank my BICHOK! warrior women, Lynda Toney-bahr and Aliza Bloom Robinson. Just knowing you were out there with butts in chairs and hands on keyboards, too, kept me moving forward. Your feedback and friendship mean the world to me. You are so inspiring and you will set the world on fire with your own writing projects.

Along with Lynda and Aliza, I'd like to thank my other early readers, Christine Sinclair, Sarah Cavender, Barbara Kelly, Linda Curry and Beata Lorinc, for their encouragement and valuable suggestions.

I'm deeply grateful to Carolyne Ruck for her astute insights in editing my manuscript. She has an amazing way of pruning the straggling thoughts and coaxing out clearer form to help the story to blossom.

Thanks to Helen Rowles, art teacher extraordinaire, for introducing me to the amazing possibilities of colored pencil art. Her guidance and patient suggestions helped me to bring my inner vision of Fallen's scenes and characters to life.

Kudos to Neal Koppes, who did a fabulous job of professionally photographing the illustrations and making them look so sharp in both color and black and white.

And huge thanks to Michelle Radomski for designing such a gorgeous and enticing cover. She took one of my illustrations and grafted it beautifully with the perfect font and filigree to bring the feeling of fairy tale adventure to life before the reader even turns the first page. Without her gentle encouragement and creative design expertise, you would not be holding this gorgeous full color Collector's Edition in your hands.

Photo credit and gratitude to Sharon Spall Photography for her gorgeous PR photos, one of which appears on the back of the book and others on Facebook and my website. The location, lighting and photographic artistry beautifully reflect the fairy tale feeling of Alora's world.

My deepest gratitude goes to my family, who always encourage me and support my creative meanderings. Ryan and Sarah, I love you to the moon and back. And, David, my dear husband, thank you so much for always supporting me in every way imaginable. I couldn't have done any of this without your unwavering love. We sure knew what we were doing when we all got together in the Dreaming Tree and decided to have this adventure together. As Blaze would say, "Woo Hoooooooooo! What a rush!"

CONTENTS

CHAPTER ONE

Spinning Dreams

Once upon a Timeless Now, in the emerald realm of the Dreaming Tree, a little leaf swayed in the gentle breeze, humming softly as she spun a new dream. As one leaf among the thousands that filled the tree, there was nothing outwardly remarkable about her. But one must never judge a leaf by her appearance, for this garden-variety, third leaf on the second bough from the bottom known as Letria was about to change everything.

As a dream spinner, Letria worked tirelessly to capture and express the thoughts and visions burgeoning within the Dreaming Tree's boundless mind. In a ritual she'd repeated countless times, she drew a deep draught of the tree's lifeblood and flooded it through the veins and capillaries that ran like a roadmap through her kelly-green, heart-shaped body. The nectar of infinite consciousness exploded within her in a kaleidoscope of flavor, color and sound that blurred the borders of her senses. She smelled the fresh crispness of sapphire blue, tasted the tang of rolling thunder and heard the sweetness of honey as birdsong.

Once the initial rush of sensory overload had passed, she began the work of distilling a single dream scenario from the infinite possibilities available. Like an artist selecting a harmonious palette of colors, she chose this bit and that from the multitude of impressions flowing through her, by intuition more than by thought. The potential combinations were limitless, and never had she duplicated a past dream.

Through a miraculous process of inner alchemy, she transformed her selected elements into a gossamer substance finer than spider silk. With deft precision she spun this into a radiant dream orb that hung, glistening, from her leaf tip.

Throughout the Dreaming Tree, other leaves were likewise engaged. Their collective web of dreams sparkled like a jeweled crown in the canopy of the tree. The harmony of their voices as they hummed and sighed filled the tree with a symphony of sound. It was the sound of Om, the voice of creation. Usually it filled Letria with a sense of peace and belonging, but lately it left her feeling edgy and restless.

She sighed deeply, the pleasure she normally took in her work offset by a vague feeling of dissatisfaction. These dreams that she spun endlessly, each one precious and unique, were so fleeting. There was no beginning, middle or end to them, for this was the realm of the always Now. Each was a complete and perfect expression, a beautiful golden light of self-contained potential, frozen and suspended for the briefest moment in the amber of timeless time. It was like a series of stillbirths, thousands upon thousands of them. Each dream was here so briefly before dissipating or falling off into the void, only to be replaced by another. They were expressions of the Great Mind, yes, but not experiences.

And so it was. And so it had always been.

But now, as Letria peered into the alluring diamond sparkle of her latest creation, a restless yearning hollowed her insides. It was a rather achy longing for something more, something she couldn't name. A flood of fierce and tender love for this creation of her heart swelled to the point of bursting within her.

As she gazed more deeply into her dream, its crystalline glow shattered into a rainbow of colors unlike any she'd ever known. The colors spilled into her as bright golden light snaked like fire up her midrib, rich violets and magentas flowed sweetly through her veins, and icy blue raised every downy fiber on her body.

She sensed, or perhaps only imagined, a flash of movement and sound within the dream orb. A tingling curiosity sent shivers through her as she trembled from stem to tip. Through the shimmering veil of the orb's surface, she thought she saw an ephemeral vision of herself within the dream.

No, not quite me, she realized; *more like a projection or reflection of me. Yet she's alive, she marveled, spellbound. I shall call her Alora, my little dream. But I couldn't bear to lose her like all the dreams that came before.*

What would it be like to live within the dream, she wondered? *To hold it for longer than a moment? To be held*

3

by it? To really experience it? The very idea of living a different kind of life than this one was so unfamiliar that she had no word for it. But the idea created a feeling of excitement within her that bubbled up and overflowed, as the answer to her question took shape in new, breathtaking language. It would be . . . an "adventure."

The alluring word "adventure" tumbled and tickled inside her like an invitation. Her heart leapt with an instant *Yes!* in response.

~~~

Up the branch from Letria, the eleventh leaf, Lexi, had just spun his own dream. He juggled the dream across his forest-green surface repeatedly, kicking it in the air with his leaf tip, catching it near his stem and letting it roll down his midrib back to the tip. He wasn't showing off, exactly, but he wanted to get Letria's attention.

He had picked up on her restlessness. As connected as they all were, it was impossible for anyone's thoughts or feelings to remain unknown to the others for long, especially those closest to each other. Lexi felt particularly close to Letria—and not just by proximity. She held a special place in his heart. Her kind and gentle nature moved him. She cared so deeply about everything. She spun her dreams with a depth of love and passion far beyond what he brought to the task.

His dreams tended to be random and wild. He relished the surprise of spontaneous creation and the unexpected

4

results of his hit-or-miss selections from the flux of the Dreaming Tree's mind. He enjoyed stretching the limits— like seeing how many elements he could bring into a single dream, or just how big he could spin an orb before it burst.

His dreams were like a field of scattered wildflowers; hers were a carefully tended garden. He let go of his dreams easily, always ready for the next experiment. But she seemed to grieve the loss of each one. He'd noticed recently that she often seemed sad and listless. He'd hoped to cheer her up with his silly antics, but she wasn't paying any attention to him.

He sent a mental message as he lobbed his dream orb one more time. *Look at this, Letria. How high do you think I can toss it?* But still she didn't respond or even look his way. She was staring into her dream orb with an intensity that worried him. He caught his tossed dream and let it roll slowly to a stop as he focused completely on tapping into Letria's thoughts.

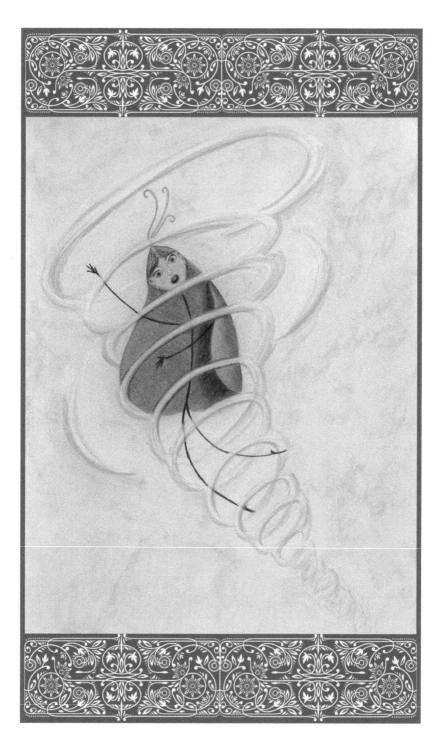

CHAPTER TWO

Falling Dreams

The word "adventure" resonated within Lexi, and the echo of Letria's resounding yes pounded like a drumbeat through his veins. As he felt her grief and longing, and her overwhelming desire to hold on to this dream—to truly experience it—he suddenly realized what was happening.

"Be careful, Letria! You're falling!" he shouted.

But it was too late. She didn't even hear him. For an instant, Letria became the dream and forgot that she was the dreamer.

In that instant, the Dreaming Tree's infinite consciousness spiraled through Letria and into her dream, refracting like rays of light through a prism. The timeless presence of the infinite Now unwound and expanded, exploding into time and space within the world she dreamt.

The love that she felt for her dream turned inside out, birthing fear and a whole spectrum of unprecedented emotions into the new world. The perfect quantum balance held in the mind of the great Dreaming Tree stretched and flowed into long threads of discrete possibilities, spanning like bridges between polar extremes of light and dark, hot and cold, good and bad. It was the collapse of the quantum wave or the big bang of a universe being born. Into the maelstrom, a fragment of Letria's consciousness fell.

Lexi watched, dumbfounded, as a phantom-like replica slipped from Letria like a second skin and passed through the thin membrane of her dream orb. As if the weight of her essence within it was too much, the dream stretched and dropped from her grasp. It fell, siphoning light from Letria as it went, bleaching her shining, spring-green surface to dull olive.

Lexi didn't waste time trying to process what he was seeing. His only thought was for Letria. She needed his help. He needed to keep her safe. Somehow she'd slipped into her dream and he had to follow her. He couldn't bear the thought of life without her.

Without hesitation, Lexi projected a bit of himself into his own dream world, willing it to fall along with Letria's. He shuddered as he felt a layer of himself slip away and penetrate his falling orb. Their two sparkling dreams tumbled and fell in a graceful ballet, like two stars locked in a shared orbit.

Letria's strange new concept of adventure swept through the canopy like a wild wind, stripping bits of consciousness from random leaves throughout the Dreaming Tree. They dove into their own dreams, which streamed like a comet trail behind Lexi and Letria's twin stars. The rogue wind, gone nearly before it had arrived, left scattered pockets of darkness throughout the canopy. An eerie stillness filled The Dreaming Tree as all the leaves within it held their breath.

~~~

Not even an instant had passed in the Dreaming Tree, but it felt like an eternity to the fallen bit of dream stuff that had spun out from Letria's consciousness.

That bit felt an unbearable pressure at the base of her stem as a great wind tore her from the Dreaming Tree. Searing pain shot through her as her stem split in two, each resulting limb fluttering wildly as she spun helplessly in the cyclone. *Legs.* The new word came into her mind unbidden. Two of her main arteries lengthened out beyond the borders of her curved sides and, with them, came the word *arms.* Up toward her tip strange new features emerged, isolating the senses she once experienced universally throughout her body and assigning each to a specific organ. *Eyes, ears, nose, mouth.* Above these, a few curly tendrils unfurled and fluttered in the gusting wind as if reaching out for something, anything, to hang on to.

Gasping and suddenly desperate for air, she inhaled deeply. The wind roared deafeningly in her ears, and her eyes watered with the sting of it. There was a dry, metallic taste in her mouth that she somehow recognized as fear. She tried to process these new sensations and to make sense of all these changes in her body as she spun dizzily down, down, down.

She lost consciousness for a moment and, when she came to, she had no recollection of her home in the Dreaming Tree. It was as if all she'd ever known was this crazy swirling wind, the spiraling of blue and green around her, and the sensation of falling.

~~~

In the Dreaming Tree, Letria awakened from her reverie with a start and shouted out, "Oh no! What have I done?"

She stared, aghast, as she watched her dream, and the sweet little leaf within it, tumble down. She called out, "Alora, my darling dream leaf, don't be afraid. You're safe, Little One. I will help you. Alora! Alora! I'm here."

~~~

In the cyclone of wind, the fallen leaf spun chaotically, completely disoriented, alone and afraid. The wind's rushing, pulsing rhythm created a distinctive sound vibration that was felt as much as heard. She fell and fell, grasping this sound as her last tenuous hold onto life itself. The sound was a name. Her name.

Alora.

CHAPTER THREE

Fallen

After what felt like a terrifying eternity of spinning and falling, Alora landed at last with a soft splash on an icy-cold body of water. Still dizzy from the fall, her insides felt unstable as she bobbed and rocked sickeningly on a vast expanse of blue. With every move she made, the water beneath her rolled and threatened to pull her under. Twice her face went below the surface, and twice she came up gasping for air.

She gave up trying to move for the moment and floated, face up, squinting her eyes at the intense light that blazed down on her from above. Besides being way too bright, the light was uncomfortably hot. It was a strange and unpleasant sensation to be sandwiched between the scorching brightness above and the cold, clammy water beneath her. While her front burned, her backside felt like it would freeze. The juxtaposition created a physical tension within her that only increased her anxiety. Her head was pounding and her heart was racing.

She slowly and carefully moved each of her arms and legs, one at a time, feeling the cold, silky water swirl around them. They seemed to be working all right. Gingerly patting her face and body, she was pleased to find no apparent injuries.

Well, she thought. *Whatever just happened, I seem to have come through it in one piece. I'm a bit shaken up, but at least I'm alive. Okay, Alora, don't panic—think. What is this place?*

In an attempt to get her bearings, Alora slowly moved into a sitting position, careful not to lean too far to either side lest she set the water rocking again. She shook her head, trying to clear it. The dizzy jumble of water, rocks and trees surrounding her felt at once foreign and familiar. She both knew and didn't know this place. *Lake Sojourn.* The name sifted through her consciousness like sunlight through the leaves of a tree.

Okay, that's good. I'm a leaf on Lake Sojourn. Now, how did I get here? As hard as she tried, she could only remember spinning wildly in a windstorm. Before that? Nothing.

A gentle breeze danced softly around her. Breathing deeply, she caught the green, resinous scent of distant trees. Somehow familiar and comforting, it triggered an intense longing within her for something she couldn't quite remember, a yearning for community and belonging. She felt strangely disconnected. *Why am I all alone?* she wondered. Tears sprang into her eyes as her heart dropped into a bottomless well of loneliness.

14

She found herself staring into the depths of the lake where vague, shadowy shapes undulated in murky water that faded away to pitch black. At some deep, cellular level, beyond thought, a connection was made between that watery abyss and the fear and loneliness she felt. In her mind she named it *The Deep,* and wanted nothing to do with its frightening mysteries.

Pulling herself together, she vowed to do everything she could to stay afloat on the surface until she could figure out how to get off the lake completely. If only she could remember where she'd come from. Would anyone be searching for her? "Hello," she shouted. "Can anyone hear me?" But she heard only the echo of "me . . . me . . . me . . ." bouncing across the empty water.

She lay back and stretched out on the water, staring up into the blue sky above, grateful that at least that glaring hot light was no longer directly overhead. *How am I going to get out of this mess?* she wondered. She kicked one foot in frustration. The cold water burned as her leg slapped against it. Her body lurched and skimmed a short distance, then spun in a lazy circle before coming to a stop. Intrigued, she tried it again, first with one leg and then with both. She had very little control over her direction—but she was moving!

She tried a similar movement with her arms, slicing them up and down, into the water and out again. Icy droplets splattered her chest and stung her eyes. The agitated water bounced her up and down until she nearly went under. Desperately trying to regain her balance, she instinctively pulled her arms under and through the water. *Oh! That's better,* she thought. Although her twiggy little arms and legs didn't displace much water, she managed to coordinate her kicking with a rudimentary backstroke that gave her a small amount of controlled mobility. It was an exhausting effort, and the direction of her movements was erratic, but her modest success did much to boost her morale.

Okay, now that I can move about, where should I go? she asked herself.

She sat up once more to scan her surroundings, trying to decide which direction looked promising. *I can't be the only one out here,* she thought.

The quality of light was changing; the sky was taking on a rosy glow. The long, shimmering shadow her body cast on the water triggered another wave of fear and loneliness. "Please," she whispered. "I don't want to be alone."

A sudden gust of wind sent her flying. She spun through the air for a few helpless moments before splashing down near some round, flat leaves. Their slender stalks disappeared into the greenish gloom beneath them. Here and there amidst the leaves, deep-purple blooms opened like hands to the sky. Tiny buzzing creatures hovered suspended in the fragrant air above the blossoms.

"Hello!" she said to the leaf nearest her. It seemed not to have heard her. She swam toward another leaf and tried again, but still received no answer. She tried once more, this time speaking to one of the flowers. "Excuse me. I'm Alora and I just arrived here. I wondered if you might help me"

Before she could finish her sentence, the blossom began to slowly gather its petals up into a tightly closed knot.

Well, that was a bit rude, she thought.

It suddenly dawned on her that these leaves weren't really like her at all. None of them seemed to have any arms or legs, unless you counted the long stems that went down into The Deep. They didn't have faces either. Maybe it wasn't rudeness—but rather, an inability to talk.

How sad, she thought, *to have so many companions around you and not be able to talk to them.*

Perhaps they were more like the water and the sky—part of the landscape, but not alive like she was. Somehow, that made her feel more alone than ever.

As the last of the violet blooms closed, the swarm of insects zoomed off and disappeared into the shadows in the distance. In the quiet that followed, a barely perceptible humming vibration caught her attention. One of the tiny creatures had fallen into the water and was frantically spinning in circles on its back. Its waterlogged wings fluttered wildly and its little legs scrambled in the air.

"Oh! You poor little dear," Alora said, her heart opening in empathy with the creature and its plight. "Let me help you." She extended her hand and felt the tickle of wee legs on her fingers. Finding purchase at last, the insect righted itself and dragged its way, dripping, up onto Alora's arm. She gently deposited it on the surface of a nearby leaf, where it sat, drying its wings for a moment, before speeding off with a happy buzz. She continued to gaze in the direction it had flown long after it had disappeared from sight.

Alora shivered. The light was fading quickly and the air was growing cooler. The evening was alive with sound. From somewhere high up and far away, she heard waves of trilling sing-song notes. Closer to hand, a chirping chorus of *ribbits* droned monotonously. Tiny splashing sounds pattered all around her as the lake's smooth surface shimmered and rippled.

Soon the sky turned as dark as the water beneath her. Once-clear shapes and landmarks faded into fuzzy shadows, and then disappeared altogether. She felt completely untethered from anything real—adrift within a pitch-black void and profoundly, desolately alone.

The chirping grew louder. It seemed to surround her and close in on her. Furtive rustlings and splashes made her heart pound. Disembodied howls, shrieks and bugling sounds echoed from somewhere beyond the shore, adding to the cacophony. Every unfamiliar sound felt like danger to her, like a nightmare she couldn't wake from.

Eventually, out of sheer exhaustion from the day's events, she drifted into restless sleep. In her dreams, the night's wild sounds became whispered voices calling her name, "Alora . . . Alora . . . Alora." She dreamed she was nestled snugly among others like her, rocking on a green sea of love and safety, soothed by the susurrant sound of whispering leaves. Her body relaxed completely and she slept deeply through the rest of the night.

When the sun woke her, she rubbed her eyes and shook her head, feeling disoriented. It took a few moments before it all came back to her—the wind, the tumbling fall and her wet landing here on Lake Sojourn. All at once, a feeling of utter hopelessness dropped like a stone within her, filling her veins with lead and draining every ounce of her will and energy. She drifted in a numb haze.

Days spun by, marked by cycles of light and dark, heat and cold, as Alora drifted helplessly upon the surface. She half-heartedly practiced her backstroke, but it took enormous energy and yielded only minimal control over where she went. By day, fickle winds blew her from one part of the lake to another. She never knew when she'd next be tossed about, and she felt completely at the mercy of the elements.

Each night she dreamed of being rocked in a cradle of green glowing light and enveloped in a sweet lullaby of sound. But even as she drifted into the peaceful bliss of her dreams, she would awaken with a start as strange shapes bumped and swirled beneath her, silver missiles in the murkiness tentatively prodding her exposed backside.

She grew more terrified of The Deep with each passing day.

CHAPTER FOUR

Catch a Fallen Dream

Before she became the Dreaming Tree, Numina had floated for time untold in solitude, suspended in the void, with only her thoughts for companions. It had been enough, at first, since every conceivable reality was contained within them. But the infinite force of love within her sought expression. Her urge had grown toward creation and manifestation—beyond thought itself, to thought made into form.

She had unfurled from formless thought like a primal seed germinating, reaching out through countless roots and branches, exploding with vibrant green life through twig and leaf. She'd flexed and stretched, reveling in the sensations of physical presence, feeling the powerful flow of love and consciousness rush through her in manifest expression of *I AM*. But still she'd been alone, and her love had sought connection.

And so she had given each of her leaves consciousness, and the power to dream—to weave her thoughts into form. She had delighted in their creativity as well as their companionship. She loved them. Together they had become the Dreaming Tree, and for another long stretch of timeless time, that had been enough.

Yet it was no surprise that one of her leaves should now wish, as she had, for more.

She watched as Lexi and Letria's fallen dreams danced in parallel, for one breathless moment, before embracing and becoming one. Other drops in the cascade of falling dreams bounced and crashed against each other, jostling the dream leaves that floated within them. One by one, the fallen dreams merged together until, at last, they all blended into a single, gigantic dream orb. The collective dream thus created tumbled toward the void in a headlong race to certain oblivion.

It would be so easy to let it fall, Numina thought. To dream is one thing. But to give the dream life? There are so many unknowns in that course.

Part of her longed to hold on to the simplicity and beauty of things as they were. But what of her leaves? Would they begin to wither and die of longing? In a way, her entire Self was like the dreams her leaves spun—a closed system, frozen in timeless time.

It's already cracking open, she realized. There can be no containment. Expansion is the inevitable evolution of love and consciousness.

In the instant before all was lost, the Dreaming Tree stretched and spread her gnarled roots, reaching out to gather the falling orb into the safety of her embrace.

Letria exhaled in relief. Lexi rustled with excitement.

A murmuring arose like a whispering breeze as leaves throughout the tree released their held breath and began to react.

"What's happening?"

"Why is the light so dim here?" "What is this strange new thing?"

"Hush. Be calm. All is well," spoke the melodious voice of Numina.

"Hear me, my children," she said, and every leaf instantly attuned to her voice as her words spread like nectar through and over their murmuring. Rarely did she speak aloud; there was no need as her energy and consciousness ceaselessly permeated every limb, twig and leaf. The soothing caress of her dulcet voice amplified the significance of what was occurring.

"All is new and all is well. I hold our collective dream safe. Our sacred circle remains unbroken. It has simply stretched and twisted into new form, an infinite winding loop."

For, indeed, the circle of glowing light that had always filled and surrounded the canopy of the tree now looped downward in a figure eight that encircled and illuminated the dream orb below in beautiful balance and symmetry.

"Letria, my child," Numina continued, "there is no fault, no mistake. Love brought your dream to life. The Fall is love's creation. Lexi, your act of following was also an act of love. What is done through love can cause no harm—yet it can change everything."

The leaves trembled and shimmered as a powerful wave of Numina's love swept through them. Those who had released a part of themselves into the collective dream felt a powerful bond of love, like a rainbow ribbon of light, connecting them to their fallen dream selves—their own light willingly dimmed to supply life to the Fallen.

"All consciousness within the collective dream is still with us; never gone, never separate," Numina assured them. "The Fallen are safe. They do not remember you. You must allow them to remember in their own way and time. You may send dreams, guides and inspiration, yet you may not choose their paths for them."

Letria gasped. While Numina's words were soothing, she couldn't help but feel responsible for all that had happened. She herself had triggered the Fall—of Alora, and of all the others as well. She had loved her dream so deeply that she'd wanted to hold on to it. And now Numina was telling her that, because of love, she'd have to let it go.

"The Fallen will feel in ways previously unknown," Numina said. "You will be tempted to protect them. Do not. For it is through these many feelings that they will come back to love and find their way home. All that they experience within the dream is a gift—not only to them, but to you—to us—as well. They are our light."

Lexi watched as Letria's already-dimmed countenance blanched even more, and his worry for her grew. He hoped that jumping after her had been enough; that his Fallen self would be able to help hers. More than anything, he just wanted to see Letria light up again.

Numina concluded, "You gave the Fallen life through love. Through love you must also give them freedom. And by love will the Fallen find their way home."

CHAPTER FIVE

Stuck in the Muck

etria watched as Alora drifted on the silver-blue surface of Lake Sojourn. Her connection to Alora was strong, but Alora remained oblivious to it. Her fear and loneliness wrapped like icy tentacles around Letria's heart. Reaching out to her with love and compassion, Letria projected soothing thought vibrations: *Alora, Little One, you're safe. You're not alone. I'm here.* She slipped into Alora's dreams each night, but couldn't seem to reach her when she was awake.

"She's so frightened," Letria marveled, as the strange and sour bite of the word triggered an intense desire to do something for Alora that would make the feeling stop. "I only want Alora to know she isn't alone; I want her to know she's safe. But I can't seem to reach her. She doesn't remember me."

Lexi observed his own dream double, Blaze, with a group of other Fallen at the edge of the lake, some distance away from where Alora drifted aimlessly. "She's not really alone. We are all in the same dream, just not in the same place," Lexi said.

"Maybe I can help her find the other Fallen so she won't feel so alone," sighed Letria. She took a deep breath and let it out slowly as she focused her energy on filling the gap between Alora and the others with all of her love.

~~~

Alora stretched and yawned as the sun rose into the morning sky, rubbing her eyes in irritation at the headache that was already brewing after another sleepless night riding The Deep. The heady fragrance wafting on the morning breeze told her she'd drifted near the floating forest of round leaves and purple blossoms during the course of the night.

Startled by a loud, jarring *ribbit,* her eyes flew open just in time to catch the streak of dull green that plopped into the lake, dousing her with icy water. She barely had a moment to register her surprise and indignation when a great, rising wall of water lifted her up and propelled her, spinning wildly, across the surface.

She sputtered and sneezed and tried to regain her equilibrium as the rippling water met the shore, depositing her in the noxious, sticky mud at the edge of Boggy Marsh.

"Hey, quit pushing me," an angry voice said.

Startled, Alora looked around. A wave of relief washed through her as she realized the voice belonged to another leaf. His scowl and gruff words did nothing to dispel the burst of joy she felt at meeting a fellow sojourner. Behind the leaf she'd jostled, a whole crowd of leaves gathered together in the mud. These were not like the mute round leaves whose long stems disappeared into The Deep. These leaves were plump and round on the bottom, pointy at the top, with arms and legs and faces just like hers. She felt an instant kinship; a sense of homecoming. Her days of loneliness were behind her. But her relief was short-lived.

A rank, sour smell rose from the mud. In it were mingled odors of stagnant water, decay, and . . . something else. *Fear,* she thought, as she noticed that most of the leaves were cowering and trembling in the mire, their eyes darting uneasily between the brush beyond Boggy Marsh and the skies above them. The reason soon became apparent as a collective shriek rose from the assemblage.

With an ear-splitting "caw, caw," an alarming dark shadow descended from above. Huge wings, black as The Deep, clapped like thunder, buffeting the leaves with an ominous wind. Petrified, Alora watched mutely as menacing black talons skimmed a hair's breadth above her before snatching the grumpy leaf she'd just met and carrying him off, screaming, into the bright-blue morning sky.

The remaining leaves wailed and moaned and gathered closer together. Not knowing which of them might be next, they hoped to find safety in numbers.

Alora's heart pounded and she tried to slow her breathing. The realization that she could have been the one snagged by those deadly talons hit her with a force that nearly knocked the wind out of her. A nauseating blend of relief and guilt roiled sickeningly in her stomach. *If I hadn't bumped into that poor fellow, he might still be safe,* she realized.

She had barely recovered when she heard the snap and crackle of breaking twigs and branches coming from the brush beyond the bank. In the space between two scrubby trees, where the earth was worn smooth by constant use, a massive antlered head emerged. Slowly the bearded brown giant lumbered toward the helpless leaves. Alora stood trembling and transfixed as one of the beast's huge cloven hooves began its descent directly toward her.

~~~

An uneasy rustling filled the Dreaming Tree as the leaves looked down upon the carnage unfolding in the dream world below.

"I dreamed up that creature with the black wings—Raven," one leaf confessed. "I thought it was sleek, strong and beautiful. I never meant it to be frightening."

"That antlered creature—Moose—that was my dream creation," admitted another. "I never imagined the damage it might cause."

"We must do something to help!" insisted a third dream spinner.

"But remember what Numina said," another leaf reminded them. "All is well, nothing is lost and we aren't to interfere. The Fallen must find their own way through this nightmare."

~~~

"Look out!" a voice shouted, as strong hands pushed Alora swiftly out of the path of descending doom. She landed with an undignified splat in the smelly mud, but out of harm's way.

The hoof missed her by inches as the shaggy brute continued on its course, trampling others of the Fallen with no regard for their shouts and cries. It stopped for a moment to drink from the clear water beyond the mud before turning to plod slowly back into the wood.

In the aftermath, she heard leaves calling for help, and she watched as their companions worked to pull them up out of the muck. Some leaves had been buried too deep to recover; others lay broken and lifeless on the ground. Alora looked on, too stunned to be of help. A dizzying freefall of emotions tumbled within her, spilling out as tears.

The same strong hands that moments ago had pushed her to safety now reached out to help Alora up out of the mud. She found herself gazing into brown eyes so dark and shining that she felt she might fall into them and drown, but in a much nicer way than she would in The Deep. Taking in his trim figure and lovely rusty coloring, she felt a jolt of instant connection. She shook her head, suddenly feeling dizzy. She had the strangest sense of watching all this from outside of herself, as though she'd seen it all happen before.

~~~

Because Lexi had entered the dream with focused intention, while Letria had fallen unaware, Blaze's fall was not quite as traumatic as Alora's. Still, crossing the threshold into time and space had felt to Blaze like being stretched and twisted through a keyhole and turned inside out in the process. He'd held on for dear life to the thought of Alora and his mission to help her. But his memories had been stretched right out of him as he fell. He'd landed in the world of Lake Sojourn filled with a sense of adventure, determination and purpose, but no memory of Lexi, the Dreaming Tree, or the details of his quest.

~~~

Now Blaze's heart pounded with adrenaline after the near miss. He'd seen too many of the Fallen trampled or carried off into the sky in the days since he'd arrived here. He'd barely been able to push someone out of the way of one of the great hairy monsters just moments ago.

As he reached down to help her up, Blaze found himself gazing into wet emerald eyes and a winsome face white with fear and worry. His whole body tingled as his hand grasped hers. As her enchanting spring-green body rose gracefully up from the ground to meet him, a wave of expansive vertigo swept through him. An instantaneous click of destiny turned a key within his heart, filling him with an overwhelming desire to help and protect, above all others, this particular leaf.

"Are you all right?" Blaze asked. "I haven't hurt you, have I?"

"N-n-no, I-I-I don't think so," Alora sniffled through tears. "At least, not nearly as much as that hairy beast could have. Oh, but those poor leaves over there! They've been trampled. And that black monster just flew off with the fellow right next to me!"

Blaze made a quick scan of the sky and the brush beyond the shore. Satisfied that the coast was clear, he turned back to Alora. He put a hand to her cheek and gently wiped away a tear. "You're safe now," he assured her, looking deeply into her eyes. "The creatures are gone, at least for the moment. I'm Blaze, by the way. I don't remember seeing you before."

Alora shivered at his touch and inexplicably felt safer in his presence. "I'm Alora. I've been floating alone out there for days," she said, waving a hand that encompassed the whole of the lake's sparkling blue surface. "I didn't even know there were others here until just now."

A sudden sense of community and belonging washed through her. *I'm not alone! There are others; others just like me,* she realized. *And right now they need my help.*

"Speaking of the others," she said, "shouldn't we try to help?"

Blaze was amazed at the sudden change in her. Just moments ago she'd had two terrifying near misses, yet her first thought after barely shaking off the mud was to go and help the others. The color was returning to her cheeks and her green eyes shone with determination. He agreed at once, and the two of them headed over to where the Fallen were still trying to extract themselves from the compacted mud.

Alora and Blaze worked together as a team, helping to pull the remaining leaves out of the muck and assess their injuries. Alora felt better almost at once. It was good to have something to do and to be helping others. It made her momentarily forget her own fears.

~~~

In the Dreaming Tree, Letria smiled as she felt the tension she'd been holding ever since The Fall ease a bit. At last, the connection had been made. Alora was no longer alone.

Lexi was heartened to see a bit of light and color return to Letria's skin. It was nowhere near her original brightness, but it was a step in the right direction.

CHAPTER SIX

Harness the Wind

The dangers of Boggy Marsh were unrelenting. The Fallen grew more and more fearful as shaggy, four-legged creatures came and went, stomping through the mud in search of fresh water, trampling any leaves in their path. Huge black birds continued to drop out of the sky and carry leaves off to line their nests. The sun baked the leaves by day, and the cold night left them shivering and sleepless in the damp mud. They clustered together in small groups, replaying the latest trauma in gory detail, grieving the friends they'd lost, cursing whatever fate had brought them here, and waiting for the next hoof or claw to fall.

While the other Fallen were frozen by fear and waiting around hopelessly for the next calamity, Blaze seemed totally fearless. He watched for patterns in the movements of the dangerous beasts and managed to always keep Alora out of harm's way. Alora was more than happy to follow his lead. She felt safe and protected around him.

~~~

Here and there in the Dreaming Tree, leaves began to regain their color and light as bits of fallen consciousness returned home.

Those who'd been caught up in the wind of Letria's adventurous imagination had fallen without conscious intention. They were the first to be trampled or carried off in the dream world below. The intensity of the experience was too much for those Fallen with no strong bond to their counterparts in the Dreaming Tree. Yet, as Numina had promised, no consciousness was lost. What seemed a terrifying death within the dream was simply an express ticket home to reintegration.

Letria knew that Alora was ultimately safe, yet at any moment she could be the next to be trampled—and her adventure would be over. She'd dreamed of so much more for Alora. "I know we can't choose their paths for them," she said to Lexi, "but it's far too dangerous for Alora to stay in Boggy Marsh any longer."

"We can't choose their paths, but we are allowed to send dreams," Lexi replied. "Maybe I can help."

~~~

Blaze had awakened from a restless night filled with strange dreams. He'd been chased by shadowy monsters which he'd narrowly escaped by gliding, nearly effortlessly, at breakneck speed across land and water. Now he sat with

Alora at the edge of Boggy Marsh listening to the familiar sounds of the Fallen's constant commiseration. "I've been thinking," he said. "It's stupid to hang around here—stupid and dangerous. Let's get out of this place."

"But where would we go?" Alora asked, startled by the thought that they might actually choose a destination. "And how would we get there anyway? This mud is so sticky I can hardly pull my feet up out of it. Besides, how do we know we'd be any safer somewhere else?"

"Well, we know for sure we're not safe here. The way I see it, we can either stay stuck in the mud waiting to get trampled, or pull ourselves up out of it and set a new course."

"I'm definitely not interested in going that way," she insisted, shuddering as she pointed in the direction of the Bramble Wood where the trampling creatures lived. "And out there on The Deep," she continued, turning a wary gaze to the blue expanse of water, "there are other kinds of monsters. Plus, the wind was always blowing me all over the place."

"That's it!" Blaze said, his dream fresh in his mind. "The wind! Maybe we can harness the power of the wind to get out of here and find someplace safe."

Alora wasn't sure she'd heard right. Was he insane? So far, the wind had only landed them all in danger. How in the world did he expect to harness the wind anyway?

Blaze set to work right away to test his theory. He twisted this way and that in the light breeze that blew, noting the subtle shifts in pressure he felt against and within his body.

If he turned edgeways to the breeze, he felt it slip and tickle around him, creating a pleasant rippling movement through his whole body, but not moving him from where he stood.

When he met the breeze face on, it knocked him backward into the squishy mud. He could feel his color rise as Alora giggled. He pushed himself up and shook the mud off. Trying again, he found he could stay standing if he dug his feet into the mud and leaned forward into the breeze to stay balanced. That was all well and good if he wanted to stay put, but he wanted out of Boggy Marsh. He wanted the wind to move him, but not knock him down.

He turned his back to the breeze and it almost knocked him face first into the mud this time. Instinctively, he rounded his shoulders back and lifted his head up to keep his balance. He felt the wind fill the curve of his back and lift him slightly. He was almost sure it would carry him forward if his feet weren't stuck in the mud.

He extracted his right foot with a slurping sound and immediately felt the pull of the wind stretch through the length of his embedded left leg as his body began to lift. Leaning back slightly, he pushed his shoulders even closer together and, with a sudden wet pop, his left foot slid free— and he was airborne.

"Woo Hoooooooooo," he shouted as he rose higher. A few feet up he began to spin, and within seconds he nosedived back to the ground, splattering Alora with the smelly brown muck of Boggy Marsh.

Alora's heart thumped with fear as Blaze crashed into the ground, but her fear turned to annoyance as he extracted himself from the mud, still grinning from ear to ear.

"What were you thinking? You could have been badly hurt," she said, throwing her hands up in exasperation.

"I'm thinking this is our ticket out of here," Blaze exclaimed spinning in circles and slinging mud everywhere. "What a rush! You've got to try it!"

"No thanks! I've had enough of the wind. Besides, how's it supposed to get us anywhere? You're still here, aren't you? All you managed to do is crash right back into the mud and splatter it all over me in the process!"

"True, but I'm just getting started. All I have to do is figure out how to balance and steer. Well, that and how to land a little better," he added with a sheepish grin.

Blaze practiced all day. He figured out, after accidentally being blown out of the mud and crash-landing into the lake, that gliding on the surface of the water made it easier to control his course and travel forward, instead of upward.

Starting in an upright position, with his legs dangling in the water beneath him, he could turn his body at just the right angle to the prevailing breeze. Then, after throwing his shoulders back and feeling the breeze fill the concave shape his body made, he would pull his legs up into a kneeling position and let the wind skate him over the lake.

He quickly learned to fine-tune his course with subtle shifts in his body, leaning or turning slightly and using his legs like a rudder to shift direction or gather speed, then

41

dropping one or both legs down into the water to slow down or stop.

Alora watched with a mixture of anxiety and amazement. She remembered the helpless feeling of being blown all over the lake at the mercy of the wind. She was afraid that the wind might take Blaze away from her, or that he might get hurt. But, here he was, harnessing the wild wind for his own purposes. Blaze was reckless and brilliant and unstoppable. He scared her to death sometimes, but she loved him.

~~~

In the Dreaming Tree, Lexi flushed with a rich russet glow, thrilled with Blaze's accomplishment.

"Well done!" Letria exclaimed, mirroring his rosy light.

A thrill of joy rushed through Lexi as Letria beamed a look of admiration in his direction.

~~~

Once Blaze had fine-tuned the art of harnessing the wind, or "windskating," as he liked to call it, he'd insisted on teaching the process to Alora. Now she sputtered and shook her head, slinging sparkling drops of water in every direction. Yet again she had landed face first in the water while laboriously trying to master this windskating that Blaze made look so easy. She hadn't yet achieved his natural balance with the wind and water, but she was determined to keep trying.

Blaze caught his breath at the beauty of her. A halo of rainbow light shone around her as the water glittered like diamonds upon her glowing skin. "You're doing so much better," he told her, biting at his lips to hold back the laughter that bubbled up inside of him. He knew that if he laughed, her eyes would spark with green fire. She might even spout off a few angry words, but her anger would be short-lived. She was always quick to forgive. Her face would soften as she joined him in laughter, and her smile would melt his heart.

He couldn't explain the strength of the feelings he had for her, or where they had come from. From the moment he'd first gazed into her eyes—was it only a few days ago?—he had felt an instant connection and fierce protectiveness. Since then, he'd spent every minute with her.

Alora laughed and said, "You call this better? I'm soaking wet and half-drowned. If this is better, I'd hate to see worse!" She felt like a complete klutz compared to Blaze. He made it look simple, and she wanted so badly to impress him. He was everything she was not: brave, smart, strong and graceful. And he wasn't so bad to look at, either. She loved the russet and golden streaks that ran through his coppery skin and highlighted his rugged physique. His chiseled face could move from frowning concentration to dazzling smile in a heartbeat, and his brown eyes sparkled with constant mischief.

She was amazed how, after having spent only a few days with him, she already couldn't imagine her life without him.

He was her strength and her compass. If he wanted to leave Boggy Marsh, she was determined to follow him no matter how many times she half-drowned in the process.

Her laughter was like music and Blaze's heart thumped to its rhythm. "Let's take a break," he said. "You can catch your breath and dry off in the sun."

The others looked on with suspicion at Blaze and Alora's activities. The general consensus was that the Fallen were not meant to carry on in such a manner. It was undignified, and it went against nature. They certainly weren't meant to go gliding around on the water, for pity's sake. No. Having landed here in Boggy Marsh, they felt it was simply their lot in life to deal with things as they were. Windskating? Bah! Blaze was reckless, and poor Alora would follow him to a bad end.

As Alora dried herself in the warm sun, Blaze went to speak to the others. "We're leaving in the morning," he said. "Anyone who wants to is welcome to join us."

A wave of grumbling and muttering gave way to one strong voice. "Go on with you, then," it said. "Make your bargain with the evil wind and leave us here in peace. We have work to do watching out for the beasts that plague us, and no time to waste on the likes of you." Murmurs of assent rose and fell like waves.

"It's a shame you're dragging that innocent girl into your insane scheme," another spoke up. "When you both drown in The Deep, it'll be you who's to blame."

That night Alora dreamed of Blaze. His eyes sparkled like starlight and his lovely scarlet and orange highlights radiated with intoxicating warmth. Seeking the comfort and safety of that warmth, she stretched her hand out to him. He reached back, calling her name. But then his warm glow flared, igniting in a flash of fiery light that quickly faded and disappeared, leaving Alora's hand reaching vainly into empty space.

She woke with a start, weeping and calling out, "Blaze! Blaze!"

"Shh. Shh. Shh. I'm right here," Blaze said, taking her hand. "You were dreaming. It's okay. I'm right here."

Relief flooded through her as his soothing voice calmed her pounding heart.

The sun was rising, shining its golden light onto her face. She squeezed her eyes shut at its brightness. *The sunlight must have triggered the dream,* she realized as it burned through her eyelids. Within seconds, the dream had faded along with her fear. She shivered with a tiny thrill of excitement as she remembered their plans for the day.

Opening her eyes wide, she turned to Blaze and said, "When do we leave?"

"No time like the present," he replied, grinning broadly. They walked out into the water without looking back. The other Fallen had made their opinions clear. There was no point in goodbyes. Still, Alora felt sad for the ones they were leaving behind. She hoped that somehow they would remain safe. Maybe, if she and Blaze did find a safe haven, they could come back and try again to convince the rest of the Fallen to join them.

Hand in hand, Blaze and Alora stepped into the cold water, harnessed the morning breeze and skated out across Lake Sojourn together, seeking the safety of some as-yet-unknown destination.

CHAPTER SEVEN

Into the Unknown

The trouble with journeying into the unknown is that it's . . . well . . . unknown. Blaze wasn't sure exactly what kind of a place they were looking for. Someplace where they wouldn't be trampled or snatched up into the sky would be nice. And someplace without any mud would be an improvement, too. But where were they to find such a place?

Alora's windskating skills had improved, but she didn't have Blaze's physical strength. Only a short time after leaving Boggy Marsh, she was already tiring.

Blaze spotted a small cove and motioned for her to follow him into it. They glided up to a shallow bank covered in tall grasses and flowers. The ground was solid. It was damp but not muddy. Blaze scanned the ground for hoof prints or feathers, spotting neither. He breathed deeply and smelled only rich earth mingled with a sweet floral scent. The fragrance was fresh and pure, unlike the musky odor of hairy beasts and stagnant water that permeated Boggy Marsh. The water, sheltered as it was on three sides by the cove, was still and not too deep, making it easy to launch back out into the wider lake.

"This looks like a good spot for now," Blaze said. "Why don't you rest up for a bit and I'll go back out to do some scouting."

Alora didn't much like the idea of being left alone, but she was tired and it was a lovely spot, so she agreed to Blaze's plan.

As Blaze set out to explore, Alora lay back in the sweet grass, its tall, slender stems surrounding her like a forest. Sunlight caught the individual blades as they danced in the gentle breeze, creating flickering patterns of shadow and light that washed over her in waves. It was mesmerizing, and soon she drifted off to sleep and into dreams.

She wandered through a shimmering world of green light that flowed all around her in veils that were almost, but not quite, solid. She saw a face. Was it someone on the other side of the green veil? Or was she seeing her own reflection? She couldn't be sure, but the eyes that looked back into hers seemed older and wiser somehow. Those eyes looked at her with such love that she felt them warming her to her very core.

"Alora, my Little One," the face said. "I am so very pleased with you. Heart of my heart, soul of my soul, know that you are safe. I am always with you—and you are always home."

Waking, she sat up and rubbed her eyes, scanning the lake for Blaze. The dream was instantly forgotten, but the feeling of it stayed with her and left her restless. She was filled with a longing for home, but she didn't know where home was.

Who am I? she wondered. *Where is my true home and how did I end up here? Not just here, in this Sunny Cove, but here in this strange world at all? Why am I here?*

She thought of those they had left behind in Boggy Marsh, and she worried about them. She was happy to be out of that place, and happy to be safe with Blaze, but she did wish that the others had come along too. Should she have tried harder to convince them? Weren't the Fallen her people? Weren't they all in this together? It didn't seem to bother Blaze in the least, but leaving the Fallen behind had left some kind of a hole in her.

~~~

Letria sighed. Alora was safe and no longer alone, and yet she still felt empty. "Do you think she relies too heavily on Blaze?" she asked Lexi.

"Without Blaze, she'd still be stuck in Boggy Marsh," he replied, slightly hurt.

"I know that, but . . ." She paused, gathering her thoughts. "Numina says we aren't to choose for them. But isn't that exactly what Blaze is doing?"

"Well, she made the choice to go with him, didn't she?" Lexi argued.

"Yes, but she's following him blindly instead of thinking for herself. She's not really finding her own way. I know you sent Blaze to help, but . . ."

~~~

"I checked out those big boulders on either side of our Sunny Cove. They won't be very useful to us, I'm afraid," Blaze reported upon returning from his first expedition. "They'd be difficult to climb, and there are large gaps between them that we could easily fall into."

"I had a strange dream while you were gone," Alora said, only half listening to Blaze's news. "I don't quite remember it, but it got me to thinking. Do you remember where you came from? Before you landed here, I mean."

"Hmm. I hadn't really thought about it," he said. "Does it matter? We're here now, so it seems that the most important thing is to learn all we can about this place."

"I just have a feeling there's something more, some reason why I'm here. Something I'm supposed to remember," she said with a faraway look in her eyes.

Blaze tapped her forehead with his finger. "Maybe you think too much," he said with a grin. "Me, I'm just here . . ." *to keep you safe,* he thought, but didn't say aloud. "For the adventure!" he concluded.

For the rest of the day, Blaze set out in one direction after another, zigzagging his way across the lake in search of the perfect place to call home, and returning to Alora at intervals with reports of what he'd found. She was content to watch him come and go and to drowse in the sweet grass and warm sun in between.

"Looks like some trees fell around the curve of the shore beyond Boggy Marsh," he said after another exploration. "The land's a little firmer there, but I think that place is already taken. There are lots of small buzzing creatures living in the logs. I don't know if they're dangerous, but I'd rather not take a chance."

"I've seen those creatures before," Alora said. "They aren't dangerous. They just buzz and fly about. They're quite small and they seem to love flowers. I rescued one of them from drowning when I was drifting out on the lake, before I found you and the rest of the Fallen."

Blaze marveled at Alora's capacity for compassion. She'd been out there all alone for days on end, not knowing any more about this strange land than he did. She had to have been scared. And yet she took the time to rescue a creature that could well have been dangerous for all she knew. Blaze felt himself flush with embarrassment. He'd been feeling like a great adventurer, like Alora's protector and hero. But she'd been even braver, just by following her heart.

"This Sunny Cove is actually very nice," Alora said. "I've been safe and comfortable here for most of the day now. The sun is warm, the grass is soft and sweet and there hasn't been a single threatening creature in sight. We could just stay here. And perhaps, after a few days, we could even go back and get some of the others."

"Maybe," Blaze replied, feeling more determined than ever to prove his worth. "But there might be someplace even better. I want to keep looking before I make up my mind."

Alora smiled at his endless sense of adventure. She was pretty sure that he'd never stop exploring until he'd investigated every inch of the lake's territory. That was all right, she thought. If there was a better place, he'd find it. And if there wasn't, at least he'd burn off some of that boundless energy of his. She got exhausted just watching him sometimes.

"There's a gigantic tree across the lake," he exclaimed, returning to the Sunny Cove once again. "Makes the trees in the scrub wood around Boggy Marsh look no bigger than these grasses. I think we should steer clear of that— there were lots of those big, black-winged creatures going in and out of it. It's starting to look like this Sunny Cove may be our best bet after all, but I've still got a few more places to check out."

Alora's eyes followed the graceful curve of Blaze's back as he windskated out into the lake once more. She lost sight of him as he rounded the boulders that jutted out from the bank to the left of Sunny Cove. Shadows were starting to fill the cove as the sun dipped low. The surface of the lake shimmered with golden sparkles as the breeze picked up in small gusts and flurries. Alora shivered as the air cooled, and hoped this would be Blaze's last trip for the day.

Blaze reveled in the feeling of freedom that windskating gave him. It filled him with an exhilarating sense of power and possibility. The sun was painting the sky in vivid shades of pink and orange, and every ripple on the lake's surface reflected the sky's brilliance. He headed off into the sunset feeling more alive than ever.

He saw Alora's gentle and trusting face in his mind and he wished, more than anything, that she could experience this same sense of oneness with the elements. He wished she could feel this freedom and power.

She had such a big heart. The way she cared so much about the other Fallen, for instance. He hoped that she had a place in her heart for him as well. He knew she looked up to him and relied on him, and he wanted so much to keep her safe. But he wished she could see herself the way he saw her; to recognize her own beauty, strength and wisdom.

A sudden gust of wind shot him forward faster than he'd ever moved before. He laughed with reckless abandon. Forgetting, for the moment, Alora and his mission to find a safe place for her, he simply savored the intense rush of the wind against his back and the water beneath his knees.

He felt no separation between his body, the wind and the water. It was as if together they formed one living, breathing being. He could no longer tell whether it was the wind or the water that moved him. In truth, it was both. For as the wind pushed him from behind, a great current rushed beneath him, pulling him forward into the setting sun.

Suddenly, the water beneath him fell away—and he was flying.

~~~

Letria knew the pain Alora would feel to lose Blaze. She felt it within herself already—the sacrifice of it, the hollow emptiness. And yet she also knew that more would be gained than lost. She breathed deeply and surrounded Alora with love.

Both the Fall and the Return were, in this timeless Now, already given, already done. Yet all that lay between, all that was contained within the ephemeral orb of the dream world, belonged by rights to Alora and the other Fallen. Their freedom was a sacred trust that must not be broken.

She understood that now. Perhaps she'd already interfered too much.

She released the dream, giving the dreaming of it over completely to Alora. But she would never abandon her. Expending all but the tiniest bit of her remaining light, she wove it through every fiber of the dream world so that Alora need never be truly alone.

Lexi watched and worried. There was a strange orange halo around Letria, and her own light had grown extremely dim. He hoped that doing what she'd asked had been the right thing.

~~~

Alora paced as she waited for Blaze to return. In the fading light of the setting sun, she walked down to the lip of the cove and scanned the entire lake, calling out his name.

There was no sign of him anywhere. A twist of fear rose from her belly to her throat, only to be pushed back down with a heated burst of anger. It was just like him to take reckless chances. And how dare he leave her alone in a strange new place?

Maybe he was out there somewhere, hurt. Or maybe he just went too far and it was too late to get back before dark. Maybe he'd come back in the morning.

She slept fitfully and dreamed again of reaching out for Blaze through empty space. Voices, male and female, spoke to her in reassuring tones. But all she wanted was for Blaze to come back. Then Blaze was there, but not there. He shimmered and radiated like the colors of the setting sun. "Come find me," he said. "But find yourself first."

CHAPTER EIGHT

Alone Again

lora woke with tears streaming down her face. The sun was just rising. She stood at the mouth of Sunny Cove and scanned the lake in every direction, searching for any clue to where Blaze might have gone. She alternately waited and paced, calling out his name time and again. But the icy feeling that pumped through her veins told her he wasn't ever coming back.

The day passed in a numb haze. She climbed into the water and floated listlessly, not bothering to harness the wind. Where would she go? She had no idea what direction Blaze had gone. She could go back to Boggy Marsh, but that seemed pointless.

She felt heavy as a stone. Part of her mind wondered why she didn't sink into the fathomless depths beneath her. Perhaps that would be for the best, really. It would be so easy just to sink and drown. The idea of going on without Blaze felt much harder.

She'd grown to rely on him for safety and companionship—and even for excitement, she realized. She would miss the reckless, exuberant, irrepressible energy that Blaze always demonstrated. He always knew what to do, and he did it with both determination and humor. He let nothing stand in his way. And while she was often irritated and aggravated by his full-steam-ahead energy, she had to admit that without it she'd still be stuck in Boggy Marsh, shaking with fear like the rest of the Fallen.

And yet, here she was, adrift once more upon The Deep, no better off than when she'd first arrived in this miserable place. In fact, it felt far worse now, measured against the warm safety of the days spent with Blaze. Without him, the time ahead loomed dark and empty. She didn't know how she would go on.

If Blaze were here, he'd know what to do. She laughed ruefully at her circular logic. "Damn you, Blaze!" she shouted as the tears began again. "What am I supposed to do now?" Agonizing, ugly sobs echoed across the water for what seemed a very long time.

Eventually she mustered up enough energy to lift her head. Searching in vain for some sign of Blaze, her eyes swept the perimeter of Lake Sojourn. Across the lake, tall reeds hugged the shoreline, and next to those a giant tree rose from the bank so high into the sky that Alora couldn't even see the top of it. Blaze had told her about that tree. He'd said it was filled with those flying creatures. She shuddered as she remembered the black wings of death that terrorized the Fallen in Boggy Marsh. Had he been taken like that?

Behind the giant tree, a Shady Wood of smaller trees grew and circled around to the side of the lake where the sun rose each morning. Some fallen trees filled in the space between Shady Wood and Boggy Marsh. Blaze had told her about that place, too. He'd been worried about the small, buzzing creatures living there. She knew they weren't dangerous, but what else might be living in the wood behind the fallen trees? Had he gone back there and been attacked or injured in some way?

Behind Boggy Marsh, the Shady Wood became more brushy and brambly. Between Boggy Marsh and Sunny Cove, she could see the tumble of boulders Blaze had mentioned jutting out of the water and into a meadow. Blue mountains rose in the distance behind them. More boulders marked the other edge of the opening into Sunny Cove. Had he tried to climb them and fallen into a deep, dark crevasse?

Beyond the boulders, to the west where the sun dropped like a ball of fire each night, the blue bowl of the sky kissed the surface of the lake in a featureless horizon that seemed a million miles away. In that direction there was no edge to the lake, no landmark to indicate distance, only vast emptiness broken by the fuzzy line of the horizon. To Alora, it looked as if the world ended at that line. And she felt as though her own world had ended as well.

The sun was beginning to set in that empty horizon. It would be night soon, and once again she could feel strange shapes beneath her, disturbing the stillness of the water and bumping up against her. She shuddered and wished that Blaze was here to protect her.

It was getting colder. And darker. Fear coiled like an icy knot in her belly. But she couldn't muster the energy it would require to harness the wind and skate back into the relative safety of the cove.

As the sky darkened to velvet blue, she heard a mournful sound from above.

"Who? Who? Who are you?"

She didn't know the answer. She didn't know at all. Adrift upon The Deep beneath the dark curtain of night, Alora felt just like the color of the sky above her: an endless, dark, empty blue.

Again the call came, "Who, Who, Who are you true? It's time you knew." One by one the stars began to blink awake and fill the sky. If Alora could have seen herself from the perspective of the Owl that called to her, she would have seen that far from being alone, she was surrounded and cradled by the light of a million stars.

"Who-who-who? Who are you? It's time to remember, Little One."

But she didn't hear Owl this time, because she had cried herself to sleep.

As she slept, she dreamed of great monsters in the water beneath her. Lumbering creatures, shaped like boulders, crashing together in great battles. The boulders had arms and legs and faces on long, snakelike necks. Their sharp eyes bored into her very soul. Other creatures flashed like fire in the water beneath her, like dragons breathing flames of orange, yellow and gold.

Terrified, she trembled in her sleep. The boulders and dragons called her by name. "Alora . . . Alora . . . Come join us in The Deep," they whispered.

She woke with a start to find the morning sun coming up over the horizon. She felt a gentle breeze stirring in the morning air. For a moment she felt relief. It was a new day. It had only been a bad dream.

But then she remembered: Blaze was gone.

So much had happened in such a short time. It felt as if she'd been here only minutes, and at the same time, it seemed she'd been here forever. An endless stream of questions trickled through her mind like falling rain. *Where are you, Blaze? Will you ever return? How did I end up in this place? Where did I come from? What am I supposed to do now?*

As the sun rose higher in the sky, she began to feel the chill of the night leaving her body and a soft warmth taking its place. She decided she couldn't just stay here, stranded and alone in the middle of the lake, for one moment more. She'd never find the answers to her questions here.

The breeze was blowing from the west this morning. She decided to harness the wind and sail toward the rising sun. Toward warmth. Toward a new shore.

"Yes, Little One," the wind seemed to whisper. "Find your way home."

Slowly, tentatively, Alora tried to remember just what Blaze had taught her. *"Curl into an upright position and let your legs dangle below you in the water. Turn your back to the wind. Round your shoulders back and point your nose in the direction you wish to go. Now lift your legs into a kneeling position and let the wind carry you."*

She began to move.

CHAPTER NINE

A Lizard's Tale

Alora glided smoothly over the placid surface of the lake, but it wasn't as easy to steer her course as Blaze had made it look. Instead of making a straight line toward the eastern bank, she found herself curving toward the rocky shore to her right.

Relaxing her shoulders and dropping her legs down into the cool water, she slowed to a stop next to a tumble of boulders that climbed like stairsteps into a meadow filled with bright splashes of violet and magenta flowers. The boulders made her a little uneasy, reminding her of her dream the night before. But these rocks didn't appear to have arms, legs or faces, so she relaxed a bit.

The water was deep and still here, and the sun felt warm on her face. The rich fragrance of the meadow and a low, droning buzz made her drowsy and daydreamy.

Scenes from the past few days replayed in her mind: all those nights alone on The Deep; the terror in the faces of the

Fallen in Boggy Marsh; Blaze saving her from being trampled; Blaze experimenting with windskating; Blaze laughing and filled with excitement; Blaze skimming out of Sunny Cove one last time.

"Oh, Blaze," she said aloud. "Whatever will I do now?"

"G'day, Miss," a small voice said, somewhere to her right, among the large stones. "Beggin' your pardon, Miss, but me name's not Blaze. I believe you've mistaken me for someone else."

Startled, Alora shaded her eyes and peered into the boulders, trying to determine where the voice had come from. At first she couldn't see anyone.

"Who's there?" she said. "Show yourself, please."

Slowly, a bit of the boulder directly in front of her detached itself, pushing upward on four short legs to reveal a streamlined body of speckled leather ending in a very long, striped tail. "G'day, Miss. I'm right here."

Alora let out a startled squeak and drew back a bit. The creature was similar to the dragons she'd envisioned in her nightmare, except for his smaller size and his color which, instead of fiery red and orange, was a dull grayish brown that camouflaged him nicely into the boulder upon which he stood.

Deciding that, by size at least, he seemed to pose no threat to her, Alora responded with a cautious but cordial, "Good day to you, sir. Who are you?"

"Why, I'm Lizard, Miss. And you?" "I'm Alora."

"Pleased to meet you, Alora. What brings you my way this fine mornin'?"

"I don't even know where to begin," Alora said. "I landed here—on Lake Sojourn that is—a while ago now. I'm not sure how, exactly. There was this wild storm, and I landed on the lake and drifted for days until I found other leaves like me in Boggy Marsh. It was horrible there! But I met my friend, Blaze, and he kept me safe. Then he figured out how to harness the wind and we left Boggy Marsh together. But now he's disappeared and I'm all alone again."

"Hoy there, Alora, that's quite a story. A very tall tale indeed!"

"It's no story," Alora protested. "That's what really happened. I'm scared, and I don't know what to do. Blaze was the smart one. I don't know how to do anything without him."

"Oh, my, yes indeed. Quite a story, my dear."

"I wish you'd quit saying that! It's not a story. It's my life!"

"Exactly! Now you've got it."

"Got what? What do you mean? My life has become a nightmare, and you keep treating it like it's just a story."

"It is, darlin', it is! It's *your* story, though, so you can change it whenever you like. Let me tell you my tale, and then maybe you'll see.

"I was sittin' here on this very rock not five days past, soakin' up the sun and warmin' meself up. I was thinkin' to meself that a lovely fly or spider would just about top off the mornin' when a great, dark shadow swept over me. Before I could race into the cracks between the boulders, a blasted

Raven swooped down upon me. You've seen 'em, right? Big black wings, sharp grasping talons and black beady eyes? Well, my story was just about up, you see. My tale was about to reach 'the end,' when I had a flash of inspiration. I didn't much like the way my tale was going, and I thought to meself, maybe it's time for a new one. Just as that Raven grabbed me by the tail, I simply let go. Of me tail that is.

"That Raven flew off with nothin' but me sorry old tail a squirmin' and a wrigglin' in its beak. And I lived to grow a new one. It's even prettier than the last one, if I do say so meself," he said, swishing his new tail this way and that for effect.

"Why, that's remarkable!" Alora exclaimed. "Now I think *you're* the one with the story."

"Well of course I am! We've all got a story. We've all got a tale, right? But when it becomes a liability, it's best to let it go," he pronounced, matter-of-factly.

"So," he continued. "You've got a story about this Blaze fella bein' the smart one, bein' the one that knows what to do next. He's kinda like the hero in your story and you're playin' the damsel in distress. Well, now that Blaze is gone, maybe you'll have to play the hero yourself. Might be that it's time you let go of your old tale before Raven has you for dinner."

Alora shuddered as she remembered just how close she'd come to being nest fodder for Raven back in Boggy Marsh. She surely didn't want to end up like that. "But what do you mean, 'let go of it'? That's what happened. It's the truth."

"See, you're thinkin' you're just in the dream and not seein' as you're the one dreamin' it. You can always write yourself a new story, darlin'. And if anything's ever goin' to change, you'll have to," said Lizard. "How did you get over here to the Boulder Steps, anyway?"

"I just did like Blaze showed me and harnessed the wind."

"Oh ho! Looks like maybe you aren't so dumb after all! Maybe you're smarter than you think. What if you stopped tellin' yourself that Blaze was the smart one and started claimin' that you are, too? Why did you come over this way instead of some other part of the lake?"

"Well, I kind of ended up here by accident. The wind was blowing from the west and the sun was warm on my face, so it seemed like east was a good way to go. But I couldn't steer all that well, so here's where I ended up."

"Nothin' happens by accident, dearie. What were you thinkin' just before you set sail?"

"I guess I was thinking I needed to do something. That I couldn't just sit and drift any longer."

"So. You decided to take action and the west wind brought you here. It brought you to me so that I could teach you about changing your tale. So here's the beginning of your new story. Part One: you are smart and resourceful. Part Two: the elements are your allies. And Part Three: you're the dreamer of your own dream, the teller of your own tale. That's a sight more pleasant and powerful story than what you started out with, wouldn't you say?"

"Well, yes, but I still don't know what I should do next," Alora said.

"Why, write your next chapter, that's what! Dream your way forward. Change your focus from what isn't working to what is. Fix one eye on everythin' good and let the other scout ahead into the possibilities of what could be. And speakin' of what could be," Lizard said, as one lazy, yellow eye lighted upon a great, fat fly, "I think I just spotted what could be me breakfast."

And with that, Lizard disappeared from sight, blending seamlessly into the contours of the boulder as if he had never even been there at all.

The visit with Lizard had given Alora a lot to think about. What kinds of things had she been telling herself that maybe weren't very helpful? Of course she missed Blaze terribly, but she didn't really know that he'd come to any harm. Just that he'd disappeared. Maybe he was okay wherever he was.

And maybe she hadn't given herself enough credit. Just because she'd let Blaze make all the decisions didn't mean she couldn't make her own.

But what did Lizard mean about the elements being her allies? Ever since she'd arrived here, she'd been scared to death of all the elements in this lake world: the big animals that trampled through the Boggy Marsh to drink, the great winged creatures—Ravens—that flew through the sky. Why, even Lizard himself had nearly been eaten by one of those. And those strange shapes that bumped around beneath the water. Surely she was right to be frightened of those!

There was the wind, though. At first she'd been at the wind's mercy. From the moment she arrived here in that crazy whirlwind, she'd been buffeted this way and that by the wind—until Blaze showed her how to harness it. The wind itself hadn't changed. But now she could steer by it. Sort of.

What about the cold dark Deep beneath her? How did that fit into her story? And if it was her story and she was writing it, why couldn't she remember the beginning? Where had she come from?

As the sun began to set on another day, once again she heard Owl asking, "Who, Who, Who are you?"

She fell asleep with that question in her head and she wondered if she'd ever remember. Or was it a question of remembering at all? Maybe it was about deciding.

That night, her slumber was peaceful. She dreamed of a sweet, green light and felt herself swaying in a gentle breeze. A primordial sound on the edge of memory vibrated through her very being. A network of shining gems gleamed and sparkled in the sunlight. She was filled with a sense of belonging.

"Who, who," softly hummed Owl from his perch in the tree. "This is who, Little One. Remember."

She woke in the morning feeling a new sense of hope. She would set out in earnest to find Blaze. She would harness the wind in every direction and explore every inch of this lake world. She would be the hero of her own story instead of the damsel in distress. No longer at the mercy of the elements, she would make them her allies. And, somehow, she would help the rest of the Fallen get out of Boggy Marsh.

She made her way back out onto the lake. Heading once more for the eastern shore, she thought about all that Lizard had said. Maybe she would never know where she came from, but she could steer her own course now and choose where to go from here.

~~~

A soft glow of yellow light washed over Letria. *She's on her way now,* she thought, feeling the fire of Alora's newfound determination warm her from the inside out.

CHAPTER TEN

Love and Fear

This side of the lake wasn't muddy like Boggy Marsh. The shore rose smoothly into the Shady Wood, not at all like the steep climb of the Boulder Steps to the south. A gently bubbling stream flowed into the lake. Alora had landed to the right of the inlet where the water was still. Smooth pebbles in earthy shades from steely gray to reddish brown sparkled like gems beneath shallow water as clear as glass.

As Alora looked into the water, she saw two large, brown eyes looking back at her. Startled, she jumped and looked up into the face of a hooved creature unsettlingly similar to those who'd trampled her companions in Boggy Marsh. She let out a shriek followed by a whispered plea of "Please don't hurt me!"

"Why would I hurt you?" asked a gentle, velvet voice. "I have only come to drink where the water is fresh and pure."

"I've seen your kind before," Alora explained, "although they were bigger and wore branches on their heads. Many of my friends were trampled under their hooves in Boggy Marsh."

"You must mean Moose. I am Deer. The male of our kind, too, have antlers, though not quite so formidable as Moose's. And not until they're all grown up," she chuckled. As she'd spoken, a miniature replica of her had shyly emerged from the Shady Wood and now peered at Alora from between his mother's legs.

"It's likely they trampled you," Deer continued, "only because on that shore, one must walk through the mud in order to get to the clear water. That's one of the reasons I choose to drink here instead. Boggy Marsh is not a good place for one like yourself to be. You're small and not easily seen. Why do you and your friends gather there?"

"It's where most of the Fallen first landed after the wind storm," Alora explained, "so they just stayed. They're afraid of being trampled or carried off, but they're more afraid of what might await them in The Deep. As muddy as Boggy Marsh is, it's more solid than The Deep. I guess it feels more stable."

As the conversation continued, the young fawn grew braver and soon he was dancing exuberantly around his mother's feet, sunlight glowing on the scattering of white speckles in his soft, russet fur.

"Fear is a strange kind of stability, isn't it?" Deer said. "The Fallen gather together in fear, covering the boggy ground so completely that there's no space for a hoof to fit between them. They build the fear up in their minds and make it more and more real. Then they end up creating the ideal circumstances to ensure that their fears come true.

"But you are different. How did you come to be here at Babbling Brook, while your comrades still tremble in the mud and muck of Boggy Marsh?"

"My friend, Blaze, learned to harness the wind and he taught me, too," Alora said. "We set out to find a safer place to stay. Unfortunately, he's disappeared. So, I'm continuing his quest to explore the territory. And I'm determined to find him, too. Maybe I can even remember where I came from and find my way home."

"So it was your friend Blaze's concern for you that brought you out of danger, and your concern for him that spurs your quest now," Deer observed. "Do you see how fear makes the world smaller and love expands it? How love makes you brave and overcomes fear? Fear separates you from the truth of who you are. And the truth of who you are is love. Love is your home."

"Mama! Mama! Who's that? Who's that?" the little one asked excitedly.

"Hush, my sweet," Deer gently admonished. "She is one of the Fallen. She's trying to find her way home."

"Is it the Big Tree, Mama? I can show her!"

"Hush, my sweet," she soothed. Turning to address Alora once more, Deer said, "You may indeed have come from the

Big Tree, for a powerful wind roared through it recently. There are many like you scattered in the meadow behind the Shady Wood. I can show you the way if you like."

But Alora remembered Blaze's warning about the many winged ones in the Big Tree. She shuddered as she remembered Lizard's story of the Raven who flew off with his tail. Her stomach clenched as vivid memories of black talons skimming over her face and the look of terror on the leaf that was snatched up played through her mind. "I-I-I don't think so," she said. "But thank you for offering."

Deer's deep brown eyes gazed knowingly into Alora's. "You overcame your fear enough to move out of Boggy Marsh and the dangers there. Your love for Blaze will draw you forward, but perhaps there are yet more fears to face before you find your way home. May your journey be safe and may you find all that you seek. But be cautious, my dear, particularly if your journey takes you to the west. There is true danger in that direction."

With that, Deer turned and disappeared into the wood, her little one dancing and chattering behind her.

Alora enjoyed riding the gentle current of the small stream where it fed into the lake. She idled away some time in daydreaming as the current swirled and twirled her around. She felt something shift inside of her, like a long, satisfying exhale of breath she hadn't even realized she'd been holding. It was that heavy stone of fear, she realized. Somehow it had simply fallen away, leaving her feeling light and full of hope.

Just having names for the frightful beasts—Moose and Raven—somehow made them, and the whole world of Lake Sojourn, a little less terrifying. It still felt frightening to think of being trampled or carried off, but having names for the creatures took away the fear of the unknown. And that, she realized, was really the larger part of her fear. Because when you knew the fears by name, when you recognized their patterns and habits, how and where and why they showed up, then you could do something about them. That's what Blaze had seen all along.

The Fallen in Boggy Marsh were so fearful, they couldn't see the possibility of exploring the rest of the lake, even though staying there put them in more danger—or at least more certain danger—than leaving would. She had felt that way, too. It would never have occurred to her to leave Boggy Marsh without Blaze's prodding. And it was only her love for him that had overcome her fear and opened up the wider world of Lake Sojourn to her.

Then, when Blaze had disappeared and she'd realized that he was really gone, she'd shrunk into herself again. She'd been sad, yes, but also terrified. And it was the fear that froze her in both body and mind. After Lizard showed her she could change her story, it had once again been her love for Blaze that had energized her to try to find him. Talk about making your world larger, she thought. *Here I am exploring the entire lake, and actually talking to creatures that would have petrified me before.*

She felt her heart open like one of those beautiful purple blossoms she'd seen in another part of the lake. In her mind's eye she saw how those blossoms opened to the morning sun and closed up tight at night. And she suddenly understood exactly what Deer had meant by fear making the world smaller and love expanding it.

~~~

A brilliant flash of green light pulsated through Letria and flowed outward through the canopy of the Dreaming Tree in soft waves. *Yes, Little One,* she thought. *Expand into love. Expand into the truth of your being, and let that guide you home.*

~~~

Alora hadn't realized that the gentle current of the inlet stream had been pushing her steadily away from the shore until she began to sense the strange feeling of The Deep beneath her once more. The sun was setting and night was beginning to fall. She resigned herself to another night sleeping buoyed by The Deep. As the stars blinked in, the gentle call came once more.

"Who? Who? Who are you?"

"I've had about enough of that," Alora shouted into the night sky. "Why do you keep asking me who I am? Who are YOU?"

"HooHooHooHoo," laughed the voice in the night. "I am Owl and it's about time you acknowledged me and my question. Who are you?"

"I'm Alora."

"That's a name, but who are you?"

"I'm a leaf. I'm one of the Fallen. I arrived here in some kind of a windstorm. I don't remember anything before that."

"That's a description. And a story. But Who Are You?" persisted Owl. "You are more than a leaf, more than a name, more than a member of the Fallen, more than a story. Do you know who you really are? It's time to remember."

With a great flapping of wings and one last "WHO!" Owl departed into the night sky.

Alora was agitated. Who indeed! Who did that great, feathered night bird think he was, anyway?

She was Alora. She was alone. She was here in this lake world and beginning to master the elements. But why couldn't she remember further back? What came before the big wind? Owl's questions had her all stirred up. Who was she, really? Who was she without Blaze? And who was she before the storm? Where did she come from and why was she here? And where, oh where, was Blaze?

She slept and dreamed again of a green glowing world with sparkly orbs that shone in the sun. A gentle, soothing sound reverberated within her and she dreamt no more until the morning light woke her.

CHAPTER ELEVEN

The Sweet Truth of Dreams

As she slept, Alora had drifted close to the shore near the fallen trees. She woke to the sound of crackling brush and breathy snuffling. Alora rubbed the sleep from her eyes and then popped them wide open, stifling a scream. A huge, shaggy-haired, black beast had emerged from the Bramble Wood and was heading straight for the large hollow log that she was steadily drifting toward. The water lapped against the submerged end of the log; in seconds she would be bumping up against it.

Swatting at a swarm of buzzing insects, the creature stuck the formidable claws of his two front feet into the end of the log farthest from her and pried it apart, grunting with exertion. His muzzle disappeared into the opening and reemerged, dripping with thick, golden liquid. He rubbed a paw at his nose and then licked it clean. Lumbering on all four legs into the shallow water, he took a great long drink to wash down his sweet breakfast.

He was close enough to Alora that she bobbed on the ripples created by his noisy lapping. Her heart was pounding so loud, she was sure he must hear it. She reminded herself that, after she'd gotten over the shock of encountering them, both Lizard and Deer had been quite helpful and pleasant. And if she was going to find Blaze, she'd need to speak up and make inquiries. Intimidated by his hulking size, and nearly overcome with the musky odor of him, she still managed to squeak out a polite "Good morning, sir."

The creature lifted his muzzle in surprise and shook his head, spraying drops of water around him. They caught the sunlight and sparkled like a thousand falling jewels. The sight enthralled Alora and reminded her of the shimmering lights in her dreams.

"Who are you?" the creature asked in a deep baritone voice that sounded more curious than threatening.

"I'm Alora," she replied, her voice trembling only slightly.

"Mmph. Pleased to meet you, Alora. I'm Bear," he rumbled with a formal bow.

Feeling the last of her fear drain away with his cordial manner, she continued, "I'm looking for my friend Blaze who disappeared three days ago. Have you seen another leaf like me? A little taller and thinner, and more of a russet color?"

"Well now," said Bear, slowly, "I've seen many leaves of many kinds in many places. But until today, I have never talked to one before. How did your friend disappear?"

"He was exploring. You see, we learned to harness the wind and he spent the day windskating, looking for a safer place to live than Boggy Marsh. He went out one last time, just before sunset, and he never came back."

"Mmph," Bear grunted, mulling this over. "In the evening time, the wind often blows into the setting sun. There is a great canyon in that direction, and the water falls over the edge. It's called Lake's End. If the wind took your friend that way . . . well. Mmph. To find your friend, you may first need to seek within."

"What do you mean, 'seek within'? That doesn't make any sense. He's out there . . . somewhere," she said, sweeping an arm to include the entire vista of Lake Sojourn.

Bear bent low to the water, peering a bit nearsightedly at Alora. With his own inner eye, he saw something in her that caused him to tilt his head in wonder. Could it be that this tiny little thing carried the power that he saw in her?

"The Dreaming within you is strong. It holds the answers you seek," he said. "Scan your inner horizons. Listen to your inner voices. Heed the dreams that blossom within you as you sleep at night, for they will show you the way."

A shiver ran through her as a series of dream images flashed in her mind: Blaze flaring in a burst of light and then fading away; the feeling of softly swaying in a cool, green world; and frightening forms in The Deep calling her name. But weren't these dreams simply the restless ramblings of anxiety and exhaustion?

"I've been having a lot of dreams lately, but I don't think they mean anything," Alora said, dismissively. "And even if they do, I don't have a clue how to figure out what that might be."

"It's simple, Little One. Begin with how they make you feel," Bear said. "Then look for how they reflect your current experience. For who is to say which is the dream and which the real world? Perhaps both are but mirrors of a greater reality. Where the veil is thin, one reality merges into the other and you can become whatever you wish to be. You can become what you truly are—a shapeshifter, a magician, a changer of worlds. Heed your dreams, for they will lead you to Truth."

"But will they lead me to Blaze?" she asked, frustrated with Bear's incomprehensible gibberish.

"If he's a part of your Truth, they will," Bear replied. "You will know the Truth when it bursts like a sweet berry on your tongue; when it floods, warm and slow, like honey through your body. You must also seek within for the inner strength you will need for your journey. Knowing where to find the honey and berries is only the first step. You may need to suffer the scratch of the bramble and the sting of the bee before you can savor the sweet reward."

"But I'm not searching for honey and berries," Alora argued, determined to keep Bear on track with the issue at hand. "I'm searching for Blaze. How am I going to find him by searching within?"

"You believe that to be your quest, Alora. And you may yet find him. But I see a bigger story ahead for you. Like me, you appear to be a solitary creature. At the very least, you've embarked on a solitary journey. Do not be fooled, however, into thinking that you are the only one changed or affected by what you experience."

Bear tapped the surface of the lake with one of his front paws. "Do you feel the disturbance my foot makes in the water," he asked?

"Of course," Alora replied, bobbing up and down in the wake Bear had created.

"Watch for a moment. Do you see how the ripples continue to flow until they meet the shore? Your landing on Lake Sojourn set a similar flow in motion. Just as the ripples created by your landing eventually covered the lake from shore to shore, you are even now creating a powerful ripple effect throughout the entire Universe by your adventures here."

Bear turned and retreated back into the Bramble Wood, leaving Alora more frustrated and confused than ever. She shook her head and rolled her eyes as a slight breeze blew down from the shore and set her to drifting once more.

What in the world did that crazy old Bear mean about greater realities, shapeshifting and sending ripples through the Universe? she wondered. And what good could it possibly do to pay attention to my dreams?

She replayed the dream scene of reaching out for Blaze and seeing him disappear in an explosion of hot, orange light. Was that light the setting sun? While she didn't understand half of what he'd said, maybe Bear was right about the evening winds blowing Blaze into the sunset. And there was another dream, too, she remembered. Blaze had told her to come find him. But how would she find him if he'd fallen over the edge of the world at Lake's End?

CHAPTER TWELVE

Seeds and Wings

lora floated lazily in the warm sun and pondered her next move. She'd been to all the places she knew Blaze had gone: the Boulder Steps, where she'd encountered Lizard; the Babbling Brook near the Big Tree, where Deer had spoken to her; and now the Fallen Trees, where Bear had befuddled her with his talk of dreams and inner visions.

She thought it strange that Blaze hadn't encountered any creatures in his explorations. He'd decided that all of those places were dangerous, but she had found wisdom and guidance there. Of course, she hadn't wanted to explore the Big Tree any more than he had. Just the thought of encountering a whole tree full of Ravens made her heart jump and her belly do flip-flops. Deer had suggested that this might be where she came from. But if that were the case, she thought she'd rather take her chances down here on the lake.

Maybe she was looking for Blaze in the wrong places. He wouldn't have gone back to the locations he'd already ruled out. She'd need to cover new territory if she was going to find him. There were a few places she hadn't yet explored— like the forest of reeds near the shore beyond the Big Tree. Maybe she should make a circuit of the entire shoreline. Or even go back to Sunny Cove to see if he'd returned.

She rocked gently on the water, a soft breeze caressing her as her body grew relaxed and limp in the warmth of the sun. Her thoughts began to fragment and drift into random words and images as she drowsily sank into sleep and dreams.

"Blaze . . ." she mumbled. They were hand in hand, skimming dizzily across sparkling water. Suddenly Blaze grew wings. Not like the black wings of Raven, but wings of fire that consumed him. He disappeared, and she was alone. Then suddenly, she was in Bear's embrace. They were running through the woods. Bramble thorns tore at her flesh. Bear placed her gently in a hollow log where bees swarmed her as honey poured from her veins. The honey filled the log and overflowed in a fiery trail of orange that spilled into the water of Lake Sojourn. She was carried by this rich stream to the middle of the lake, and left to float upon The Deep.

~~~

A great burst of indigo light flashed through Letria, illuminating the Dreaming Tree with images from Alora's dream. Lexi and the other leaves watched in fascination, fluttering with anticipation.

~~~

Roused from her slumber, Alora realized that she had indeed drifted while she slept. Sitting up and stretching luxuriously, she caught a flash of orange and red, like flames, in The Deep beneath her. Looking more closely, she was entranced by the gracefully flowing tail and fins swirling just under the surface.

Two of the creatures jumped into the air, one after the other. Their white and orange scales flashed brilliantly in the sunlight. As quickly as they had appeared, they were gone, slicing back through the water with barely a splash.

They're beautiful, she realized. *Why did they frighten me so much? How wonderful it must feel to flow so gracefully and peacefully.* She remembered the warm, silken feeling of honey flowing through and around her in her dream. *Perhaps it feels like that,* she thought, longing to have such grace and beauty herself. "But how can they breathe in The Deep," she wondered aloud?

Two round, whiskered mouths emerged from the water, giggling musically. "We are Fish, silly. We are made to breathe in The Deep. Perhaps you are, too." With another mirthful laugh, they slipped beneath the surface and disappeared into the shadowy depths.

In that same moment, a great form rose up like a mountain beneath her and lifted her out of the water. She struggled to keep her balance on the hard, curved surface. From the front of the moss-covered mound, a weathered face at the end of a long, leathery neck stretched and twisted to turn a variegated eye on her. "Hello, Alora, I've been waiting for you."

"You have?" Alora asked, startled. "Who are you? How do you know my name? And what do you mean you've been waiting for me?"

"I am Turtle. I've been watching your journey, Little One, and waiting for the moment when you'd be ready. You've learned much and grown much. Your love for your friend, Blaze, has become powerful and selfless. In your search to find him, you've begun to discover your own wisdom and strength. You've listened to the wise counsel of the creatures that have come to you. You are ready now."

"What do you mean, I'm ready? Ready for what?" "It is time to enter The Deep."

Alora's heart raced. Enter The Deep? What did this talking mountain mean? The entire time she'd been here, she'd never been more frightened of anything than the great Deep upon which she floated. It was cold. It was wet. It was dark. It was completely unknown. It was nothing like this surface world that she'd become so adept at navigating. "I-I-I can't possibly enter The Deep," she said. "I'll drown. I'll die."

"The answers you seek are there," replied Turtle. "Trust the journey. Trust yourself. Look at me—I can navigate both The Deep and the surface. In fact, I must navigate both in order to survive and thrive. The Deep lives within me even as I emerge into the surface world. The Deep feeds me, but I must surface to breathe. Let me take you to another who can demonstrate the power of The Deep to you."

Turtle began to swim across the lake toward the tall reeds next to the Big Tree. He carefully kept the topmost portion of his shell above the water to keep Alora dry and calm. They soon reached the thicket of cattails, and Turtle stopped.

"Look—do you see?" Turtle asked.

"I'm not sure," said Alora. "I see the reeds . . . Oh!" She gasped as she noticed what Turtle meant. The cattails were alive with glimmers of brilliant blue and orange. Phosphorescent wings sparkled and danced in the sunlight.

"Oh!" she said again. "They're beautiful! What are they?" "Dragonflies," replied Turtle. "You're seeing them in their most evolved form, at the apex of their lives. Yet before they gain their wings, they live more than half their lives in The Deep."

Turtle made a strange little chirping sound and one of the flying gems came and landed on his shell, close to Alora. The rich electric blue of her segmented body was decorated with intricate patterns in brown and black. Now that the wings were still, Alora could see there were four of them, as wide as the creature's body was long. She could see straight through them, yet at the same time they seemed to hold all the colors of the rainbow.

"Hello dear," came the tiny, melodious voice as Dragonfly turned her bulbous eyes from Turtle to Alora. "Welcome to Dragonfly Thicket."

"Alora is here to learn about The Deep," Turtle said to Dragonfly. "Can you tell her how you got your wings?"

"Long ago," Dragonfly began, "my mother planted the seeds of her highest hopes for the future into The Deep." Dragonfly swooped down and skimmed the water gracefully, coming to rest on a green leaf blade just above the surface, drawing Alora's eyes downward. "I was born in The Deep in a very different form than what you see today. The Deep nourished me as I grew. One day, I fell asleep and I dreamed of a new world."

In a dizzying flash, Dragonfly zoomed upward and then quickly nosedived to come to a hovering halt at eye-level with Alora. "I emerged from that dream with wings, and claimed the upper realm as my home. Now my domain is the air—and yet I remain inextricably tied to the realm of The Deep. Like my mother before me, I will plant seeds for the future into The Deep."

Landing once more on Turtle's back, Dragonfly continued, "You see, the seeds of our future must know The Deep. They cannot be planted in the air. They must be fed by The Deep to thrive. Perhaps it is the same for you?"

"I don't know—I'm just a leaf. I don't think I have any seeds to plant," Alora said, puzzled.

"My wings do not allow me to journey beneath the water," said Dragonfly, "and so I must release my seeds from above, letting them drop into The Deep and trusting them to emerge when the time is right. But you have no such impediment, Alora. You can dive deep to discover the seeds of your own power. If you are to gain your own wings, you will find them there, in The Deep. Turtle is the perfect guide. Follow him and you will find what you seek."

CHAPTER THIRTEEN

Deep Dive

As Dragonfly zipped away, Alora marveled at the story she'd told of planting seeds in The Deep and growing wings. While she didn't completely understand everything Dragonfly had said, Alora could feel the wisdom and truth in the creature's words. *Maybe The Deep's not all that bad if creatures like Dragonfly emerge from it,* she thought, as she watched the ephemeral flashes of color darting in and out between the cattails. She sat entranced by the sight until Turtle harrumphed.

"What? Oh, I'm sorry, were you talking to me?" she said.

"Indeed I was," said Turtle. "I was saying, can you see now that The Deep is an important dimension of your experience? Within it, you will find the answers you seek— and the strength and wisdom to find Blaze."

As Alora pondered Turtle's question, he turned and swam slowly away from Dragonfly Thicket, taking her back toward the deepest part of the lake. Her heart beat faster at the thought of diving into The Deep. She remembered how, when she'd first landed here, it had terrified her; how it had seemed to hold all of her deepest pain and loneliness. She could still feel the choking sensation and the burning in her nose from the times she'd briefly gone under, trying to master windskating. And that was only in the first few inches of water. How could she possibly dive deeper and survive?

"I'm afraid," Alora said. "It's one thing to plant seeds in The Deep, but you are asking me to do the impossible."

"No, Little One, not the impossible. I'm asking you to face your deepest fear, to embrace it and to dive into it. For this is where your answers lie. I can take you. Are you ready?"

Alora trembled with a sudden chill that was at odds with the sunny sky. Her mouth was dry and her heart pounded. She'd been terrified of The Deep ever since she'd arrived here. But she did want to remember who she was, and what had come before that great and terrible wind. More than anything, she wanted to find Blaze. If he were here in her place, she knew he would dive without hesitation. But she wasn't daring like Blaze. *"Now that Blaze is gone, maybe you'll have to play the hero yourself,"* echoed Lizard's distinctive voice in her mind.

But all this talk of seeds and wings is ridiculous, Alora thought. And I'm not going to find Blaze under the water. I'm finally learning to manage on the surface of this strange world, and that's challenging enough. I should just stick to my plan to search for Blaze up here.

"Do you see how fear makes the world smaller?" Deer gently admonished.

Other words in other voices filled her head. "Who are you true?" Owl demanded. "Come and find me. But find yourself first," Blaze insisted. "Take heed of your dreams," rumbled Bear.

She'd been dreaming earlier, just before Turtle lifted her up off the water. The honey that flowed from her own veins had carried her out to The Deep. And when she'd awoken, the mysterious shapes of The Deep had been transformed from something frightening into beautiful Fish—so lovely, graceful and inviting. Every one of the creatures she'd encountered—Lizard, Deer, Bear and Turtle—had been as frightening as Moose and Raven in its own way. And yet as she had listened to them, she'd found that they weren't so frightening after all. They'd become her friends and wise guides. So maybe The Deep would be the same? Maybe Turtle was right that the only way past her fear was through it.

Turtle promised answers—answers about Blaze and answers about who she was and where she came from. That was what she'd set out to find. It didn't make any logical sense that she'd find her answers in The Deep, but somehow she trusted Turtle and believed him. *"Listen to your inner voices,"* reminded Bear.

She got very still, closed her eyes and listened. What she heard was the buzzing of the bees from the hollow log in her dream. As she breathed deeply and grew calmer, the buzzing shifted to the sound of humming. Thousands of voices blended harmoniously in an ethereal symphony of sound that filled her with an aching longing for home. Tears of yearning spilled from her eyes, dripped down upon Turtle's back and rolled gently into The Deep.

"All right," she said, the words barely a whisper. She took a deep, settling breath.

She slid down Turtle's shell and onto his neck, wrapping her arms and legs around it as tightly as she could.

"All right," she said again, this time with strength and conviction. "Let's go!"

"Hang on," said Turtle. And he dove.

Alora held her breath and closed her eyes as she felt the silky water rush around her. She was still terrified, but there was something underneath her fear as well. A profound sense of safety, like a bubble of protection, surrounded her. She peeked out through one eye. Then she opened both eyes wide. It took a moment for her eyes to adjust, but soon she could see quite clearly through the water. What had seemed so dark from her perspective on the surface was actually filled with beautiful bands of streaming light. She felt as though she were floating in a dream.

"You can let go now," said Turtle. "You are safe. Seek your answers." As Turtle swam away, Alora felt the last remnants of fear transform into the bubbly effervescence of excitement.

She was surprised to find that she'd never felt more in her element. She could breathe, somehow. She could see and hear clearly. Why, she could even hear through every fiber of her body. She felt her body shift subtly and adapt to the new environment of The Deep. Her flat, narrow form expanded somehow into a rounded but streamlined shape. She was surprised to see beautiful gold and orange folds draping from her body like a beautiful gown. *What is happening to me?*

She heard Bear's guttural voice in her mind. *"Where the veil is thin, one reality merges into the other and you can become whatever you wish to be. You can become what you truly are—a shapeshifter, a magician, a changer of worlds."*

I know what's happening! she was astonished to realize. *I'm shapeshifting!*

She had become a Fish—one of the "dragons" she'd been so afraid of until she'd seen them jump and heard them giggle, telling her that perhaps she, too, was made to breathe in The Deep. Her now-graceful body navigated effortlessly through the water. She could swim in any direction she chose. It felt a bit like when she'd learned to harness the wind—except here, in The Deep, she needn't wait for the wind to come from a particular direction to get where she wanted to go. Here she was completely in harmony with her environment. She glided effortlessly, this way and that, getting a feel for her new form and enjoying the sensation of freedom as the water caressed her silken scales.

She easily covered large distances. She traveled to the places she knew, stopping first to let the water tickle her body in the shallow flat where the Babbling Brook fed the lake and Deer had taught her about fear and love. She swam past the fallen trees in front of the Bramble Wood where Bear had told her to look within, and on past Boggy Marsh to the Boulder Steps where Lizard had helped her to claim a new tale.

She drifted into Sunny Cove where she and Blaze had briefly escaped the terrors of Boggy Marsh. She continued along the curve of the shore heading west, but soon she felt a very strong current that began to pull her forward, faster than she wanted to go. She remembered Bear's warning about the water falling into a deep canyon and decided to pull back, for now. She suspected Blaze might be somewhere off in that direction, but she needed to learn a little more before she went blindly ahead into dangerous waters.

As she distanced herself a bit from the pull of the rushing water, she regained her own power and direction. She sat still for a moment, trying to decide what to do. She remembered how Dragonfly had spoken of planting her seeds in The Deep.

She swam to Dragonfly Thicket and wove her lithe body around and through the bed of cattails where she found the Nymphs who were the offspring of Dragonfly. She tried to tell them they would become flashing jewels with wings way up above the surface, but they thought she was crazy. Their lives were here, in The Deep. Why, they'd never heard of such a thing as the surface.

Alora realized that we can't always know what we'll become. But she felt a stirring within her. *Why, look at what I've become,* she thought. *I never could have imagined entering The Deep, much less changing my form so completely. If someone had tried to tell me before, I would have laughed at them, too.*

She swam away from the Nymphs slowly, pondering her own amazing transformation. The Dragonflies remembered their Nymph stage, but the Nymphs in The Deep couldn't imagine their Dragonfly future. She clearly remembered the leaf she'd been on the surface before her deep dive. But why couldn't she remember who she was before the great wind?

She heard an echo of Owl's question within her mind. *"Who? Who? Who are you?"* Her heart filled with a powerful longing to know—to remember.

~~~

Letria felt the pull of Alora's yearning in her own heart. She breathed deeply, her full focus and intention fixed on helping Alora to remember. Her exhale channeled the song of the Dreaming Tree and wove it through the water in which Alora swam.

~~~

From within Alora's powerful longing to remember, a sound arose. She felt it more than heard it. It was like the humming that had come to her in the stillness of her inner listening—a beautiful sound that filled and surrounded her, like the fragment of a dream vaguely remembered. The sound arose within her, yet she could feel it vibrating through the water around her as well. It was as if her heart were calling out for something, and the answer was echoing back from The Deep.

She dove deeper still, moving toward the sound as it grew louder. She could hear it with both her ears and her body, and with her heart, somehow, too.

She followed the sound down and down, to the silty base at the deepest part of the lake. A labyrinth of thick, snaking roots filled the lake bed. She swam between and around the roots and the sound filled her entire being. Every cell of her body vibrated with awareness and memory. Her half-remembered dreams rushed back to her clearly now, dreams of a green universe filled with sparkling droplets of light. *It wasn't a dream,* she realized! *It was home!*

~~~

There was great rejoicing in the Dreaming Tree as Letria called out to Alora and Alora heard her clearly. A river of sparkling violet light opened up between Letria and Alora and spilled over to light the entire canopy. Lexi exhaled in deep relief to see his friend's light, and her bright green color, fully return.

~~~

Alora wept with joy at the feeling of love and belonging that swept through her. All this time she'd felt so alone, so abandoned. But it was never true. This world, this beautiful green universe, and her very soul, Letria, had been there all along. She had just forgotten. But now that she remembered, nothing would ever be the same.

"Letria," she called, "I remember! I remember! I know who I am! Who *we* are. We dreamed the most marvelous dream and I chose to fall, to find adventure, to forget and to remember. I chose to become the dream."

"Welcome home, Little One," came the reply from Letria. "I am so proud of you. You've learned so much and loved so much."

"It's been you all along, hasn't it? Leading me to Lizard and Turtle and all of the other wise animals so I could find my way home. I was never really alone, was I?"

"You found your own way, Little One, through your own courage and wisdom. So many times I wanted to save you, but then you wouldn't have been free. You had to find your own way. Yet I was always with you. I am always with you. We are one."

"But what about the rest of the Fallen? And Blaze!" Alora exclaimed. "He's disappeared and may be in trouble. I have to find him! And all the others; I have to help them, too. Will you help me, Letria?"

"Yes, Little One. Whenever you call on me, I'll be there," Letria assured her. "Do not fear. All of the Fallen, like you, are safe. For they, too, are a part of us. Yet each of you has your own path to follow, your own journey through the dream, your own challenges to meet and your own magic to discover. Some paths will cross while others may never meet. Some paths converge as you choose to dream together for a time. And, after a while, those paths may split and continue on in separate directions. It is your choice, and yours alone, where your path leads. And I will be with you every step of the way."

"But I didn't choose for Blaze to leave me," Alora exclaimed. "I wanted him to stay with me!"

"I know, Little One. I know," Letria soothed. "And yet Blaze, too, made a choice. It may be hard to understand, but his choice was made from love."

"Then I choose to find him again," Alora proclaimed. "And to help all the others as well."

"If you seek to find Blaze within the dream of your world, you must leave The Deep and return to the surface, bringing all that you know and all that you are back with you. It is only there that you will be able help the others as well."

"But, how can I go back? I've been completely changed by my journey into The Deep."

"You've left the surface of the dream and awakened within it," Letria explained. "You have become a Deep Water Leaf, fully aware of who you really are. Yes, you have changed—and more deeply than you may yet realize. You will bring all of those changes, including your new shapeshifting ability, back to the surface in service of awakening others to who they are. It was love that sent you, love that awakened you, and it will be love that brings you home. Go now, Little One. Return to the surface. Your journey continues, and I am always with you."

CHAPTER FOURTEEN

Shapeshifter

lora followed the roots to where they climbed the steep bank toward a part of the shore she hadn't yet explored. She rose slowly to the surface and found herself at the base of the Big Tree. She leaped a few times, still in her Fish form and reluctant to give it up. On her third leap, she shifted. She slipped gently and easily back into Leaf form and breathed air again as if for the first time.

She felt as though she was awakening from a beautiful dream. Floating lazily on the water, she stared up into the Big Tree, where green leaves danced in the sunlight. *Was Deer right?* she wondered. *Is the Big Tree my home? It seemed different in my dreams somehow, but could this be where I came from?*

She heard Letria's voice in her heart, *"Not exactly, Little One. The Big Tree is but a reflection of your true home—a gateway of sorts between your world and mine. Everything within your world began with a thought in the mind of the*

Dreaming Tree. Everything reflects this larger reality. But it is you, Alora—you and the other Fallen—who bring it to life and dream it forward."

She would go back, she decided—back to Boggy Marsh where she would tell the Fallen who remained there that it was their own fear that was causing the danger. She would try to help them remember who they were and where they came from. She would help them to see that they had a choice in how they would dream this world forward.

But would they listen? Or would they still prefer the certainty of their fear-based convictions to the mad tale she told of her discoveries in The Deep? Would she have listened, she wondered, when she too was where they were? In truth, Alora had believed as much as they did that she was at the mercy of the elements and an unkind fate. And because she'd believed it, she'd continued to see evidence of it everywhere she looked.

When Raven had swooped down and carried off some poor, startled leaf to who knows where, she'd assumed a certain and painful death. She'd cursed Raven for its cruelty. When Moose had stomped carelessly through the mud to get to fresh water, crushing the Fallen in its wake, she'd felt fear and anger about its callous behavior.

But gentle Deer at the Babbling Brook had opened her eyes to a new reality. Because the Fallen lived in fear, they were frozen there in the mud and muck—stuck in the most dangerous place they could be! Their fear created, or at least increased, their danger—bringing about the very thing they feared most.

Once Alora and Blaze had decided to leave Boggy Marsh and harness the wind, they hadn't faced that danger again. No more smashing hooves or piercing talons. Because of their love for each other they were able to face their fears and journey into unknown territory, together. By trusting the wind to help them, they were able to leave their fears behind.

Oh, Blaze. Where are you now? I miss you so much. Why did you have to leave me? Suddenly, she thought she knew. *You left so I could find myself.*

Alora realized that it was Blaze's disappearance that had sparked her journey and led her to meet all those wise animal teachers and friends. When she had faced the one thing she feared most and journeyed into The Deep, she'd discovered that far from being the end, it became the beginning of something bigger. It led her to the great joy of remembering—and gave her the power of shapeshifting.

She thought of Lizard's story of dropping his tail, sacrificing it to Raven, and growing a new and better one. A new tale. A bigger story. What would her story be, now that she'd returned from her adventure in The Deep and rediscovered who she was and where she came from? That was Blaze's gift to her. Her own Bigger Story.

Alora had a sudden insight. While she probably wouldn't have listened to any other leaf (except maybe Blaze) who tried to show her how her own fears were creating the danger, she did listen to all the animal guides who'd come to her: Lizard, Deer, Bear, Turtle, Dragonfly and even Owl. And when she'd gone into The Deep, she'd magically shapeshifted into Fish, a form that served her better in that watery realm. Maybe she could go to the Fallen in Boggy Marsh in a different form. *Maybe then they'd listen,* she thought!

If she went to them as Deer, they'd be too frightened to listen to a creature so similar to Moose. Bear would be even more frightening with his huge, shaggy body and sharply clawed feet. Dragonfly would be less intimidating, but her tiny voice might not project well enough to be heard. Lizard was small enough, but there was no dry land for him in Boggy Marsh. Owl would be too much like Raven.

But Turtle could manage in the mud. Alora had listened to Turtle, and he had convinced her to do the one thing she was most frightened of. Perhaps, as Turtle, she could convince the Fallen to leave Boggy Marsh.

Could she take the form of Turtle? Perhaps a slightly smaller version of him so as not to appear too threatening to the Fallen?

She swam out a little way from the shore so she'd have plenty of room. She closed her eyes and called into her imagination the great, stone-like shell, the long, leathery neck, the mottled eyes, the clawed, webbed feet, so like Lizard's on a larger scale. She remembered Turtle's gentle voice and felt his wisdom. She recalled his ability to navigate both realms—The Deep and the surface.

Alora took in a deep breath and let it out slowly. She hummed as she breathed, creating within her the sound of creation that filled the Dreaming Tree. She listened with her whole body and soul until she heard it as clearly as when she'd rested among the roots in the silty lake bed at the bottom of The Deep. She breathed in the sound and felt it in every cell. She breathed in the presence and spirit of Turtle; she called out from her heart: *Help me, Letria. Help me to shift. I ask this in the service of the Fallen who are still in danger, still in fear, still asleep and disconnected. I ask this in the service of Love.*

She breathed again, deeply, and felt the shift begin. Her flat, nearly two-dimensional form began to expand. Her back rounded out and her shoulders came forward, quite the opposite of her windskating stance. Her belly hardened. Her arms and legs swelled and lengthened. Her face began to stretch upward. What an odd feeling to have such a long neck! She'd never really had a neck at all as a leaf. Even in her Fish form there had been no distinguishable separation between head and body. She stretched her neck out long, and drew it back in tight, all the way inside of the shell she'd manifested. She relished this strange and delicious new feeling.

She dove deep into the lake to practice her swimming skills in the form of Turtle. She found it nearly as easy and graceful as it had been when she was Fish, although her body was quite a bit heavier now.

Alora rose to the surface and breathed in the air, realizing that while she could remain submerged for long periods as Turtle, it wasn't the same as Fish. She couldn't actually breathe under water in this form. She thought this would be true for her in her natural leaf form as well. The Deep would feed her and live within her, but her breath and her work would be found on the surface.

Right now her work with the Fallen was waiting for her. She swam off through the silky blue water toward Boggy Marsh. She remembered her first arrival there—the elated surprise of finding others like her followed swiftly by the horror of flapping wings and stomping hooves. She felt once more that dizzying spark of connection that had flashed between her and Blaze as he'd helped her up out of the rank mud. *I will find you, Blaze,* she affirmed, *but first I have a job to do.*

Arriving at the shore, Alora dragged herself up onto the soggy bank, spreading her webbed toes wide to avoid sinking into the mire. But before she could take another step, she felt something happening within her. Turtle's form was slipping away—she couldn't hold on to it. She looked down and saw her own skinny legs and pointy feet standing inside of Turtle's much larger footprint.

She panicked. *I thought shapeshifting was my new power! I thought I was supposed to use it to help the Fallen. What good is it if I can only shapeshift in The Deep? What will I do now?*

Yet even though Alora had returned to her own natural shape, she could feel a difference in her body. She could still feel some of the strength of the armor that Turtle wore and, beneath that, the flowing gracefulness of Fish. Having embodied them, even for a short time, she felt that she would carry them within her from now on.

She realized, then, that it wasn't about the outer form as much as the inner and outer qualities. Fish was completely at home in The Deep. Turtle could bridge the worlds of The Deep and the surface. Turtle could stick his neck out, knowing that he had the safety of his shell to retreat into if necessary. Each of her animal guides had its own qualities, its own strengths, its own special wisdom. The true magic of shapeshifting was not to become the other physically, but to embody those qualities within herself.

In order to truly help the Fallen, she would have to remain one of them. She would have to return to them as Alora—her new self, not the poor, helpless girl who had left with Blaze. She was still one of the Fallen, but she was no longer a fearful surface leaf. She was now a Deep Water Leaf. She was living her own Bigger Story. She would return to them with Owl's knack for probing questions, Lizard's skill for storytelling, Deer's gentle and loving nature, Bear's dream wisdom, Dragonfly's story of transformation and Turtle's world-bridging qualities.

She would still need Turtle's help for what she had in mind, though. She didn't have the physical strength to carry out her plan alone. *Letria, I need your help,* Alora silently beseeched. *Get a message to Turtle. Tell him to come to Boggy Marsh and wait just offshore for my signal.*

Not much had changed since she'd been gone, it seemed. The Fallen were still gathered there, still trembling and grumbling while scanning the sky and the brush for the next invasion. They were fewer in number than when she'd left, she was sad to see.

She slowly walked toward them, fully herself, but somehow feeling bigger and stronger than she ever had. Standing tall and confident, she could almost feel her head lifting high above her shoulders on Turtle's long, leathery neck. "Hello. I'm back," she said, her voice projecting a bit more loudly than she'd intended.

A flurry of nervous questions rustled through the gathering as the startled leaves turned in her direction.

"Alora? Is that you?" "You look different."

"Where've you been all this time?" "Are you hurt?"

"Where's Blaze? We were sure you'd both come to a bad end."

"Calm down. Calm down everyone," Alora said. "I'm fine. Blaze . . . well, Blaze isn't with me right now. But I came to help you—if you'll let me. This place—Boggy Marsh—it's the most dangerous place on the lake, and it's your own fear that's keeping you here. When Moose comes to drink, he has to trample over you to get through this bog for fresh water. When Raven sees all of you gathered together, he can't resist the easy pickings for his nest. As long as you stay here, you are in danger.

"But there are other places," she continued, "lovely places, places in the sun, places where a gentle current can tickle your belly, places where you might feel truly at home and safe. I know there are, because I've been there. Are you ready to rise above your fear and leave this place of danger?"

A rustling murmur circulated through the Fallen like wind through a tree. Alora could feel their thoughts moving back and forth between the fear of staying and the fear of going. That was the problem. It was fear either way. As long as they continued to volley back and forth between the fear of present circumstances and the fear of the unknown, they would remain paralyzed. *"Fear makes the world smaller and love expands it,"* whispered Deer in her mind. Could love draw them forward?

"Let me tell you a story," Alora said. "Once upon a time, there was a leaf in a big, beautiful tree. She was happy there. And she loved to dream. She dreamed so well that she dreamed herself right out of that tree and into a strange new land. At first, everything was frightening. But she had one good friend. How many of you have a good friend?"

The murmurings shifted in tone as the Fallen began to turn to those they counted as friends. Pairs and triads and larger groups began to gather together in acknowledged camaraderie. The mood lifted, as Alora knew it would, because friendship is a form of love, and when love is present, fear is diminished.

"The leaf in my story found herself in the exact same place you all are in now," Alora said. "She was sick and tired of the muddy mess she was in, and frightened of being trampled or carried off. But she was even more afraid to venture out of the muck. That is until her friend, who loved her, saw that her fear was putting her in danger. So he overcame his own fears and showed her the way out. Turn to your friends. Do you want to see them get hurt? Or do you want to help them find safety?"

The little groups of Fallen turned to one another and they found that their concern for each other was greater than their fear. They wanted to help each other out of this muddy muck, this dangerous place.

They were still afraid of the unknown. But they didn't want to see anything bad happen to one of their friends. They'd already seen far too much of that. Their concern for their friends outweighed their fears. Soon a number of voices could be heard, saying things like, "We should go and find safety," "A sunny space sounds nice," and "Let's go together, my friend."

Now, Letria, Alora thought. *I need Turtle to join me now.*

As Turtle slowly lumbered up from the water and across the mud toward Alora, the nervous rustling started back up.

"What's that?"

"Have you ever seen such a thing?" "Does it have teeth?"

"Alora! Behind you! Watch out!"

"Calm down, everyone. Calm down," Alora said, in a voice that rose above the anxious murmurs. "Until now, you've only seen frightening creatures. You thought that they were bent on your destruction, but you were simply in their way. I am here to tell you that there are many marvelous creatures in this world, helpful creatures filled with wisdom. I've learned a lot from them. Turtle is one of those wise creatures, and he is my friend."

She wanted to tell them all about her journey, everything she learned from each of the animals, and all that she'd experienced in The Deep. But she knew they'd have to make their own journeys, in their own ways. Still, she could help them along.

"I trust Turtle with my life—and with yours. Remember, there are safer places for you and your friends. Don't let your fear keep you stuck in this muck. There's a bigger world out there! There are so many beautiful places. Rise above your fears and leave Boggy Marsh now—if not for yourself, then for those you love. Anyone who is ready can ride Turtle's back to one of the places I told you about. Who is willing?"

There was a bit of rumbling, and more than one sideways glance at Turtle. After a long pause, the first leaves hesitantly stepped forward. Alora was surprised and encouraged to see it was the very pair of leaves who had spoken out the most adamantly against them when she and Blaze had decided to leave Boggy Marsh.

Turtle moved out into the shallow water and submerged just enough to make it easy for the two Fallen to climb upon his back.

"Where would you like to go?" Alora asked, climbing aboard Turtle's shell with them.

"We like the sound of that Sunny Cove you mentioned," one of the leaves said. "Where the ground is dry and there are no dangerous creatures."

She gave Turtle directions and helped the Fallen to remain calm as he swam across the lake. Turtle and Alora safely deposited the couple in the tall, sweet grasses and left them to dream a new life for themselves.

Turtle and Alora began to ferry the rest of the Fallen, in twos and threes, out of the muck and into safer spaces.

Some chose to float at the base of the Boulder Steps, and Alora introduced those leaves to Lizard. "Be sure to tell them about your tail," she said, as Turtle turned to carry her back to Boggy Marsh.

Several leaves wanted their bellies to be tickled by the cool Babbling Brook and those she introduced to Deer, admonishing them to listen well to what Deer could teach them about love and fear.

Some wanted the sweet life in the Bramble Wood, so she had Turtle take them there. She asked Bear to teach them how the prickles and pokes of life could be exactly what led to the honey tree or the juicy berry. She knew he would also talk to them about dreaming, inner voices and finding your own Truth. She hoped they would try to understand and listen more closely than she had. She knew now how important those lessons were to a nourished soul and a happy life.

Others thought it sounded lovely to lie upon The Deep and gaze up into a sky full of stars each night, so she had Turtle carry them out to the center of the lake and gently submerge beneath them, leaving them floating on the surface. She knew that Owl would watch over them and gently guide them to remembering who they really were. Maybe one day, Turtle would return to take them diving.

They took some of the Fallen to Dragonfly Thicket to see the beautiful flying gems. Alora asked Dragonfly to tell them how they must plant their seeds, their hopes for the future, into The Deep—and trust them to emerge and take wing when the time was right.

Some of the more adventurous wanted to find their own way, so Alora taught them, as Blaze had taught her, how to harness the wind. She warned them of the dangerous precipice at the west end of the lake and the rushing water that could carry them over the edge. But she trusted them to be safe and to find their own way to the perfect spot and the perfect story for each one of them.

Only a few stayed behind, still too frightened to venture out into the unknown. She felt sad for them, but she couldn't force them. She could only hope that someday, some other voice from within or without would reach them and coax them out of the muck of their own fears.

She knew, too, that whether they ever left the muck or not, whether they were trampled or carried away or simply sat there and decayed, they were always, always embraced and loved by their larger soul self, the one that had dreamed them into being. No matter what happened here, they would find their way home.

"Take me back to the Big Tree, Turtle," Alora said. "Whatever comes next for me, I want to start there."

~~~

The Dreaming Tree was flooded with a beautiful blue light as Alora fully claimed her story and used it to help the others. Flashes of yellow and green burst like fireworks, lighting every remaining dark pocket in the canopy, as the Fallen chose love over fear and claimed the power to choose their own destiny.

CHAPTER FIFTEEN

Eagle's Flight

Turtle left Alora at the base of the Big Tree and bid her farewell. She climbed wearily into the curve of a root that nestled into the bank just above the waterline. She felt safe and warm there, and somehow closer to Letria. *We did it, Letria,* she thought. *We got the Fallen out of Boggy Marsh. I'm not sure what comes next, but I'm ready. As long as you're with me, I'm ready.*

She yawned and stretched drowsily, her thoughts turning to Blaze. How she wished he were here to share all she'd learned and experienced. While she no longer felt desperate to find him in the sense that he might be in danger (for she knew that he, too, was a part of the dream of the Dreaming Tree and therefore whole and safe), she did dreadfully miss his presence in her life.

As the sun set and darkness came, she slept in the embrace of the Big Tree and dreamed of Blaze.

"Who," called Owl. "Who indeed. A mightier Who than even I knew. You have conquered The Deep, Little One. Are you ready to fly?"

She only vaguely heard the words as they drifted in and through her dreamless sleep.

In the morning, she was roused by dappled sunlight filtering through the canopy of the tree. Maybe she was still dreaming, but she thought she saw a smile flicker in one of the leaves above her and her heart quickened. *Letria,* she thought, *is that you?*

She sat on the bank beneath the Big Tree and gazed down at her reflection in the water. In that reflection she saw courage, beauty, grace and love. She smiled a little bit at herself, leaned down a little closer and fell with a plop into the water. She came up sputtering, and thought she heard laughter coming from the tree.

She floated out into the deeper water, out from under the shelter of the Big Tree. She thought of Blaze with love and longing.

Gazing up into the cloudless blue sky, she watched as a dark pair of wings circled and glided, slicing through the air the way she remembered sliding through the water in her Fish form. She wondered what it must feel like to fly, and what could be seen from way up there. *What kind of creature owns the sky?* she wondered.

As if in answer to her pondering, the bird suddenly swooped downward, diving toward the water with alarming speed. She didn't think it was Raven, for it flew with a different kind of strength and grace. Where Raven was black as night, this bird had a white head and tail. Still, she couldn't help but tremble as the giant bird approached.

Eagle landed gracefully just a few feet away from Alora on a partially submerged root.

"Oh, my," exclaimed Alora! "You are much bigger close up than you appeared to be from way up there."

"As are you, my dear," chuckled Eagle. "I have a very keen eye, and I can see much as I ride the air currents, but for a moment I mistook you for a Fish. It's not often I make a mistake like that."

It was Alora's turn to chuckle as she said, "Very recently, I was a Fish! Perhaps a bit of it still shows."

If Eagle was surprised by this revelation, he didn't show it. He simply cocked his head to the side and appraised her with one sharp, yellow eye.

"You must be the one Owl told me about. Alora, is it?" "Why, yes," she replied, both surprised and honored that Owl would think enough of her to mention her by name to one as regal as this.

"You've done much for your community. You've traveled far and deep. You've rediscovered who you are and claimed your power to shapeshift. There's just one thing, I believe, that you've not yet accomplished."

"You mean finding Blaze, don't you," Alora said. "Yes, that is what I set out to do. I seem to have gotten sidetracked from that, though. While I miss him terribly, I'm no longer so afraid for him. I would still like to find him if I could, but it's not quite so urgent."

"I can help you, if you like," said Eagle. "You have conquered The Deep. Are you ready to fly?"

A shiver of excitement rippled through Alora and she realized how closely aligned, physically speaking, the feeling of fear was to the feeling of excitement. Just weeks ago, when she first arrived, would she have responded with excitement to a giant bird with huge, sharp talons, a wicked-looking beak and sharp, yellow eyes? While she might have imagined being carried off by those talons, it would have been with a sense of terror rather than the fluttery anticipation she felt right now.

"Yes!" she exclaimed without hesitation.

Eagle spread his giant wings, lifted off and flew in a great circle to gain momentum before swooping low and gently lifting Alora with his talons.

And they were off, soaring, climbing higher and higher. Up, up, up. It reminded Alora of her arrival, but in reverse. Now, as then, she felt the wind rushing by and the bright blue sky spinning dizzily around her as Eagle flew far above Lake Sojourn.

"Look down," said Eagle. "We're directly over the Cascading Falls at Lake's End now."

Alora gasped with astonishment at what she saw: a thundering, crashing veil of water dropping over the edge of the world that she knew and cascading down hundreds of feet into the canyon below. If Blaze had sailed over that, how could he have survived? Her heart sank a bit as she thought of her beloved friend being slammed into the roiling vortex of foamy water at the base of the falls.

Eagle continued flying, and he carried Alora high into the sky above territory far beyond the confines of the little lake she knew and had grown to love. She gazed with wonder at the many other lakes dotting the landscape, and wondered if each of them had their own Big Tree to connect them to the Dreaming Tree.

Eagle swung in a wide arc and began to follow the river that flowed west from the base of the waterfall. As he flew, he said to Alora, "Lake Sojourn isn't the only Deep there is to conquer. Your friend Blaze journeyed on to a much larger Deep. If you are to find him, it will be there. It's called Ocean," Eagle explained. "It's not nearly as small or as still as Lake Sojourn."

Alora could barely comprehend the vast expanse of water beneath them. Rolling swirls of azure, green and indigo, highlighted with frothy bands of white that sparkled in the sunlight, extended in every direction farther than the eye could see. All the way to the horizon, there was nothing but the blue of a Deep beyond imagining. If Blaze had journeyed into this Deep, she stood no chance of finding him. And yet, when she thought of all she'd learned and discovered in her own little Deep, she knew that Blaze was having an amazing adventure.

She called out at the top of her lungs, "Godspeed, Blaze! I love you! Visit me in my dreams and tell me all that you're discovering." And she laughed out loud. As she did, the emerald realm of the Dreaming Tree lit up in a rainbow of light unlike ever before.

"Take me home, Eagle," she said. "I've seen all I need to."

She had Eagle fly her back to the spot where she'd slept the night before among the roots of the Big Tree.

As she slept that night, she dreamed of her flight with Eagle. But in her dream, she became Eagle. She felt the graceful power of his strong wings, the keenness of his amber eyes, the sharpness of his talons and the curve of his yellow beak. She felt the wind slide around her as she claimed the sky.

In her dream, she flew higher and higher. Up and up and up. She saw the Dreaming Tree holding a blue-green orb in her roots, as Eagle might hold a fish in his talons. She flew higher still and saw many more Dreaming Trees, each with a world in its roots—trees and trees beyond counting. It was like the Shady Wood, but on an infinitely vast scale. There were Dreaming Trees without end, each dreaming its own collective dream.

Higher and higher she flew, until each of the thousands of Dreaming Trees shrank down in size, smaller and smaller and smaller. She was flying through a star-filled sky now, and each of the stars was held by a Dreaming Tree. Still she flew higher. She flew toward what appeared to be a barrier of some kind, like a glass wall.

She was able to fly right through it. And now, another bird joined her in flight, a bird with wings of fire burning orange and gold. The tips of their wings touched as they flew in unison. The barrier began to curve away beneath them. On they flew. The barrier became a round, glowing orb, cradled in the roots of a massive Dreaming Tree and filled with a million, billion stars.

She laughed and cried at the immensity of it all. The infinite forms of the One Consciousness. Dreams within dreams within dreams. The choice to fall and the power to remember. The freedom of adventure. And the gift of being both Dream and Dreamer. The Truth burst sweet within her heart and flowed, warm and slow, like honey through her body.

Dragonfly Thicket

Lake's End

Big Tree

Shady Wood

Babbling Brook

Lily Pads

Hollow Log

Bramble Wood

The Deep

Sunny Cove

Boulder Steps

Boggy Marsh

Lake Sojourn

CPSIA information can be obtained
at www.ICGtesting.com
Printed in the USA
LVHW071137171118
597405LV00008B/12/P

9 780982 105627